Queens of Romance

A collection of bestselling novels
by the world's leading romance writers

Sara Craven says:

Thank you to all my readers for sticking with me over the past thirty-three years. I've had a wonderful time, and I hope you've enjoyed it too.

THE MARRIAGE TRUCE

BY

SARA CRAVEN

MILLS & BOON®
Pure reading pleasure™

First Published in Great Britain 2002
Large Print Edition 2008
Harlequin Mills & Boon Limited,
Eton House, 18-24 Paradise Road,
Richmond, Surrey TW9 1SR

© Sara Craven 2002

ISBN: 978 0 263 20689 0

Set in Times Roman 16½ on 17½ pt.
82-1008-49379

Printed and bound in Great Britain
by Antony Rowe Ltd, Chippenham, Wiltshire

CHAPTER ONE

'ARE you telling me that Ross is here—staying in the village? That he's come back and you didn't warn me?' Jenna Lang's face was ashen, her eyes blazing. 'Oh, Aunt Grace—how could you?'

'Because we didn't know until a couple of days ago—not for certain.' Mrs Penloe's kindly face was crumpled with worry as she looked pleadingly back at her niece. 'I thought—I hoped—it was just a bit of village gossip, and Betty Fox had got it all wrong. After all, it wouldn't be the first time.'

She shook her head. 'It never occurred to me that Thirza could really be so insensitive…'

'Ross's besotted stepmother—in whose eyes he can do no wrong?' Jenna's voice was icy with bitterness. 'The woman who blamed me for the break-up of our marriage? Oh, I can believe it.'

'I suppose she's bound to be loyal,' Mrs Penloe said, trying to be fair. 'After all, he was only seven when she married his father—another one with too much charm for his own good,' she added grimly. 'And that's sure to create a bond. Although that's no excuse for what she's done...'

'What's Thirza doing back in Polcarrow, anyway?' Jenna demanded. 'I thought she was supposed to be spending the whole year in Australia.'

'Too hot and too many insects,' her aunt said distractedly. 'Or so she claims. Interfered with her inspiration. She came back about three weeks ago.'

'Brilliant timing.' Jenna laughed shortly and mirthlessly. 'She always knew how to pick her moments.'

'She claims she had no choice.' Mrs Penloe hesitated. 'Apparently Ross's been really ill—picked up some ghastly virus on his last trip. When he was discharged from hospital he needed somewhere to recuperate.' She sighed. 'Knowing Thirza, I don't suppose she gave Christy's wedding, or your role in it, even a second thought.'

'No,' Jenna said bitingly. 'I'm the one who'll have to seriously reconsider.'

'Oh, Jenna, my dear—you're not going to leave—go back to London?' Mrs Penloe asked anxiously. 'Because Christy would be devastated. And it's all my fault. I know I should have said something. I suppose I hoped it might all—go away.'

'Or that I might never find out?' Jenna asked ironically. 'Hardly likely when Thirza will probably bring him with her to the wedding.'

'Oh, Jenna—surely not even Thirza...'

Jenna shrugged. 'Why not? She's capable of anything. And I presume she's been invited?'

'Well, yes, but we never thought she'd come. We thought she'd still be in Australia.' Mrs Penloe ran a hand through her greying curly hair. 'Oh, what a mess. Why couldn't Christy have chosen a June wedding instead? Ross would be long gone by then. And the weather would have been better, too,' she added, momentarily diverted by the threatening sky with its ragged, hurrying clouds framed by the drawing room window. 'Not that it matters, of course, compared with the sheer *embarrassment* of Thirza's behaviour.

'Surely she could have found a good nursing home somewhere—and don't tell me that Ross can't afford it, for he earns a fortune and probably has the best health insurance money can buy. Or she could have looked after him in his own home—wherever that is now. Anything rather than this.'

'Maybe it isn't too late for that, even now,' Jenna said slowly. 'Do you think Uncle Henry would talk to her—persuade her?'

'Darling, that was the first thing I thought of. All he said was that Thirza might be his cousin but she was a law unto herself and always had been.' She drew a long breath. 'Also that he had enough on his plate with the bills for the wedding, and that as you and Ross had been divorced for two years it could be time for you both to move on.' She paused, giving her niece another pleading look. 'And I suppose, in a way, he does have a point.'

'I'm sure he's right,' Jenna said. 'But, unfortunately, it's a point I haven't reached yet. Because it wasn't just the divorce...' She stopped, biting her lip.

'I know, dearest, I know.' Mrs Penloe hunted for a handkerchief and blew her nose. 'So much sadness—and no one could expect you to forget...'

'Or forgive.' Jenna's voice was stony. She got to her feet, reaching for her brown suede jacket. 'I'm going for a walk, Aunt Grace. I need to think, and some fresh air might help.'

'Fresh air?' Mrs Penloe echoed. 'It's blowing a force eight gale out there.'

But her protest fell on deaf ears. Jenna was already heading out of the room, and a moment later Mrs Penloe heard the front door bang shut.

She sank back against the sofa cushions and indulged herself with a little weep. She had every sympathy with Jenna, but she was also the mother of a beloved daughter who was getting married in three days' time, and who might find herself walking up the aisle of the village church without her only cousin in attendance behind her.

Grace Penloe was not a violent woman, but she felt strongly that if she could have got her hands round Thirza Grantham's throat she would probably have strangled her.

Meanwhile, Jenna was striding through the garden, her face pale and set, her tearless eyes staring rigidly ahead.

Spring had come softly to Cornwall that year, and then, suddenly and maliciously, reverted to winter with driving showers of hail and sleet, and gales that sent the seas battering at the coastline.

The Penloes, who'd built Trevarne House on the headland that tapered into the Atlantic, had protected their grounds from the prevailing winds with high stone walls, but Jenna chose not to remain within their shelter.

Instead, after a brief battle with the heavy latch, she pushed open the tall iron gate at the end of the garden, and stepped out on to the short, stubby grass of Trevarne Head itself.

As she turned to pull the gate shut behind her the wind tore at her loose knot of chestnut hair and whipped it free, so that it streamed behind her like a bright, silken pennant.

For a moment she paused, trying to subdue it into a braid, then realised her fingers were shaking too much so gave up the unequal struggle and walked on, digging her hands into the pockets of her jacket, her head bent and shoulders hunched as she met the full force of the wind.

She had the headland to herself. The hurrying clouds and harsh wind had kept other people away, but for Jenna the weather suited the bleakness of her mood.

Long before she reached the small concrete observation platform which had been built into the turf she could feel the icy spray from the sea chilling her face, tingling against her skin, and paused, gasping for breath.

She would not, she decided, go any closer to the edge. She was not prepared to risk the odd, erratic gust which might carry her over to the sharp rocks and boiling surf far below.

She might be upset. She was certainly angry. But she was sure as hell not suicidal.

She gripped the back of the bench seat, which was bolted to the platform, and looked at the dramatic panorama in front of her.

The sea was alive and furious, streaked in grass-green and indigo as it flung itself against the granite promontory. She could hear its boom and hiss as it raced up the inlet that divided Trevarne from the cliffs of Polcarrow itself, then fell back in frustration.

Lifting her head, she watched the sea birds that swooped and dived, and rode on the waves.

Tossed by fate, she thought ironically, as she was herself.

And she had not seen it coming, although she couldn't say she hadn't been warned.

'Are you sure you want to do this?' Natasha, her business partner, had asked, her slanting brows drawn together in a concerned frown. 'Isn't it asking for trouble?'

Jenna shrugged. 'Christy and I promised each other years ago that she'd be my brides-maid and I'd be hers. She kept her side of the pledge. Now it's my turn, and I can't let her down.' She paused. 'Nor would I want to.'

Natasha gave her a wry look. 'Not even when it's the very same church that you were married in?' she queried. 'With all the mem-ories that's bound to entail?'

Jenna bit her lip. 'It's a very old church,' she said quietly. 'And I'm sure a lot of happy marriages have been celebrated there, so it will have good vibes, too.'

'Well, it's your decision,' Natasha said. 'But I helped pick up the pieces the first time, re-member, and I don't want to find you back at square one for the sake of a family wedding.'

Jenna lifted her hands. 'That's all in the past, I promise. Now all I care about is the present—and the future.'

Brave words, she told herself now, staring sightlessly at the grey horizon. And I might—

just—have got away with them. If only Ross hadn't come back...

She couldn't believe the pain that had seized her—torn at her when she'd heard the news of his return. Or how easily her carefully constructed edifice of control and self-belief had crumpled.

She wasn't suffering from some reality bypass. She'd always known it was inevitable that she and her ex-husband would meet again one day. But she'd hoped desperately that the meeting would be far, far in the future, when she might finally have come to terms with his betrayal of her.

Yet it seemed it was to be here and now—in this remote Cornish peninsula which she had always regarded as her personal haven.

It was to Trevarne House that she'd come as a scared ten-year-old after her mother's death, to the care of her aunt and uncle, leaving her father free to assuage his own grief by abandoning the desk job he hated and roaming the world as a troubleshooter for the giant oil company he worked for.

And here, on her mother's soil, she'd put down faltering roots in the Penloes' kind, easy-going household, while she and Christy, both only children, had found in each other the sister they'd always wanted.

And when, a couple of years later, her father had been killed in a freak accident when his car tyre had burst on a tricky mountain road, she had been absorbed seamlessly into the family as another daughter of the house.

All the same, she'd thought long and hard before accepting Christy's invitation to the wedding, in spite of their childhood vow. Eventually she'd allowed herself to be swayed by the knowledge that Thirza Grantham, the only potential fly in the ointment, was on the other side of the world.

Where Ross himself was to be found had been anyone's guess. She went out of her way to ignore the scraps of information that filtered through concerning his whereabouts.

Impossible, of course, she'd discovered, to cut him out of her awareness completely. To forget, as she longed to do, that he'd ever existed. For that she'd need some kind of emotional lobotomy, she thought broodingly.

Besides, there was evidence of him everywhere. The photographs which he sent back to his agency from every trouble spot in the world were still winning him prizes and awards with monotonous regularity.

'It can't be a real war,' someone had once joked. 'Ross Grantham isn't there yet.'

No, his profile was far too public for her to be able to exercise any kind of selective amnesia where he was concerned, and somehow she had to live with that.

It was strange, she thought, that she hadn't run into him in London before now. On dozens of occasions she'd thought she'd glimpsed him on the street, or across busy restaurants, even among the interval crowds at the theatre, and had felt the swift wrench of panic deep in her guts, only to realise, belatedly, that she was running scared of some complete stranger.

But then wasn't that what Ross himself had always been? she asked herself with bitter irony. A charming stranger who had murmured words of love to her, slept with her, given her for a few ecstatic weeks the prospect of motherhood, then abandoned her to pursue a casual affair while she was still recovering from the pain and trauma of her loss.

She sank her teeth into her bottom lip until she tasted blood. That was forbidden territory to her now, and she would not go there.

She'd persuaded herself that, with Thirza away, Polcarrow would be safe enough. That Ross would not come visiting unless his stepmother was there—had, indeed, not been back since the divorce.

Only, unpredictable as ever, Thirza had returned…

And as a result her life had been sent spinning once more into confusion—and fear.

Although there was no reason for her to be scared of any confrontation, she told herself defiantly. She, after all, had been the innocent party in the collapse of their brief ill-starred marriage. It was Ross who'd been the guilty party—the deceiver—the betrayer.

He, she thought with sudden savagery, was the one who should be afraid to face her.

And maybe that was true. Perhaps he was equally disturbed to hear she was in the vicinity. Just as reluctant to undergo their eventual meeting.

Because, sooner or later, it was bound to happen. Polcarrow was too small a place for them to be able to avoid each other, even for a short time.

Although Aunt Grace had said he was ill. Too ill, perhaps, to leave Thirza's house?

Jenna shook her head, almost derisively. No, she thought. That couldn't happen. Impossible to imagine Ross as a sick man. To see that strong, lithe body suddenly vulnerable, aware of its own humanity. To hear him forced to acknowledge personal weakness when he didn't even know the meaning of the words.

When he had nothing but contempt for people who gave way to their emotions, no matter what the reason.

No question, either, of him tactfully pretending to be more ill than he was to dodge any possible confrontation.

Ross, she thought, her mouth twisting, had always erred on the side of brutal candour—as she had such bitter cause to know. No white lies or cover-ups. Just the truth, coldly told. Whatever the cost...

I should have known that, she told herself. Should have realised that, once the layers of charm, intelligence and sexual charisma were peeled away, I'd find ice at the core.

I suspected it years ago, when I first met him. How was it I could be more perceptive as a child than a woman?

Well, she knew the answer to that. As a child, her thinking hadn't been muddled by the treachery of love—the bewitchment of sexual desire. And yet...

She'd been just thirteen when Thirza had been widowed and returned to take up residence in the village. And it was only a few months later when her stepson Ross had paid her a first visit.

He'd been twenty-one then, and had already embarked on his high-flying and successful career as a photojournalist.

A tall, self-contained young man, black-haired and tanned, with eyes as dark as a moonless night. And as impenetrable.

Nor was he conventionally handsome. His straight nose was a fraction too long and his eyes too heavy-lidded for that. But the high cheekbones and the firm, sensuous mouth were exquisitely chiselled, and when he smiled Jenna, for one, felt her heart turn over.

'The looks of a fallen angel,' Aunt Grace had commented privately, her lips pursed. 'And trouble down to his handmade shoes.'

But Jenna and Christy hadn't considered him troublesome at all. From the first moment they'd been open-mouthed at the sight of him, bowled over by the aura of easy confidence and sophistication that clung to him. Starry-eyed at this answer to all their burgeoning adolescent dreams, who was even—oh, joy—some kind of distant cousin by marriage. Unable to believe that for all this time they had been barely aware of his existence. But Thirza herself had been hardly more than a name to them either.

They'd been more than ready for breathless, unequivocal hero-worship—had Ross Grantham shown any sign of wanting their adoration.

But he hadn't. He greeted them with a cool civility bordering on indifference, and then appeared oblivious to their existence for the remainder of his stay.

Even after all this time, and in spite of everything that had happened since, Jenna could still wince at the memory of the lengths they'd gone to in their unavailing attempts to attract his attention.

Christy, who been reading Jane Austen's *Emma*, had bewailed the fact that all her shoes were slip-ons, and she couldn't stage an encounter by breaking a lace outside Thirza's cottage.

Jenna had had notions of persuading one of the amiable hacks they rode at the local stables to bolt with her when Ross was passing, so that he would be obliged to save her.

But before she'd been able to put this daring plan into action Ross had gone. He'd called briefly at Trevarne House to say goodbye, but the girls had been taken shopping in Truro by Mrs Penloe, so they'd missed him. And he had left no message for them either.

'Beast,' Christy had said hotly, her pretty face pink with indignation. 'Well, good riddance to him.'

Jenna had said nothing, aware only of a curious mixture of emotion churning in the pit of her stomach. Her almost agonised disappointment at his sudden departure had warred with an odd relief that such an unsettling presence had been removed, and her life could resume its usual placid path.

Except that, in retrospect she could see it never really had. Ross had remained there, a shadow in the corner of her mind, never completely banished, even though it had been seven years before she saw him again, and when they finally met it had been miles away in London.

He'd been back to Cornwall, of course, during those years. He'd come regularly to visit Thirza—never alone, and rarely bringing the same girl twice, which had set local tongues wagging. But his visits had invariably taken place at times when Christy and Jenna had been away, first at school, then at college, pursuing their respective courses.

She suspected that this had probably been quite deliberate, because they'd made such pests of themselves the first time around, but Ross had always insisted it was just a coincidence.

And she'd believed him, just as she'd somehow convinced herself that someone who so clearly liked to play the field could change and become focussed and faithful.

Because he'd made her think that all that time he'd simply been waiting for the right woman to come into his life. And that she was that woman.

She'd let herself believe too that his wanderlust—the need to be where the action was—could be subdued, that he could be tied down to a desk job, running the agency in London, even though she had the example of her own father to warn her how unlikely this was.

Perhaps if he'd lived he would have uttered a word of caution about how hard it would be for a man who'd enjoyed Ross's kind of freedom to be suddenly fettered by domesticity.

Her aunt and uncle, when she'd told them the news, had the other concerns.

'Are you really sure he's the man for you, darling?' Mrs Penloe's brow creased. 'It's not just an extension of that silly crush you once had?'

'Oh, don't remind me.' Jenna shuddered, blushing a little. 'And this is entirely different. As soon as I saw him again—I knew. And it was just the same for Ross. As if we'd always been waiting for each other.'

Her aunt pursed her lips doubtfully, exchanging glances with her husband. They'd enjoyed a happy and tranquil marriage, based on affection, respect and shared interests, and in her heart Grace Penloe believed that was the right basis for a sound relationship.

'Well, it all sounds very romantic,' she said at last. 'But I have to tell you, Jenna dear, that Thirza's marriage to Gerard Grantham was volatile, to put it mildly, and no one should pretend otherwise.'

Jenna nodded. 'Ross told me about it—and that's why he's waited to settle down. Because he didn't want the same thing to happen to him. He needed to be sure.' Her voice quickened easily. 'And now we've found each other—and we are.'

Mrs Penloe looked as if she wanted to say more, but the blaze of happiness in her niece's clear hazel eyes seemed to forbid any such thing, so she sighed soundlessly and kept quiet.

Memo to self, Jenna thought, biting her lip as she remembered the exchange. Stop thinking I know best and occasionally listen to the people who love me, like Uncle Henry, Aunt Grace, and Christy. And Tasha, of course, who'd had reservations from the first about Jenna's new relationship.

Tasha maybe most of all, she thought. Because I owe her so much.

They'd met originally through work. Her art course completed, Jenna had found a job in a smart London gallery, where Natasha Crane was already working. She was several years older than Jenny, tall and slim and striking, with black hair drawn severely back from her face. At first Jenna had found her manner faintly chilling, and had been in awe of her new colleague, but eventually there'd been a thaw and they'd become friends. So much so, indeed, that, both unhappy with their flat-sharing arrangements, they'd moved into a place of their own together.

The gallery had been a successful one. The owner, Raymond Haville, had had a sure eye for talent, and a good commercial sense, but he'd been nearing retirement and basically indolent, preferring to leave the day-to-day running of the business to his assistants. In many ways this had been a baptism of fire for Jenna, but she'd soon found herself gaining confidence and enjoying the challenge.

'We make a good team,' she'd once said buoyantly to Natasha, who'd nodded thoughtfully.

'Something we should bear in mind for the future, perhaps,' she'd returned.

But shortly after that Ross had come back into Jenna's life, and it had seemed as if her future was certain—settled, and all else had been forgotten.

Until, of course, her new world had come crashing down in ruins around her, and then, suddenly, Tasha had been there for her, strong and supportive, and offering a different kind of hope.

Raymond Haville was finally giving up, she'd told her, and her elderly godfather had also died, leaving her his antiques business, which had seen better days but was based in excellent premises.

'So why don't we go for it?' she'd urged. 'Pool our resources and open our own gallery. Raymond will let us use his contacts, and we know more than he does about the admin side.'

At first Jenna had been reluctant, unsure whether she was ready to cope with such hectic demands on her time and energy, but Tasha had been firm.

'I think it's exactly what you need,' she'd said. 'Something to take your mind off—everything else. I know you still need to grieve, honey,' she'd added, more gently. 'But you won't have time to brood. So, let's give our team a chance.'

So, almost before she knew it, Jenna had found herself a partner in a modest gallery, selling paintings, pottery and small sculptures. And discovering success.

Ross had moved out of the house they'd shared, and disclaimed any financial interest in it, so Jenna had sold up. Impossible to remain there alone, haunted by her delusions of happiness. She'd bought a smaller place, investing the surplus funds in the business and giving herself an equal stake with Natasha.

So now, two years on, she had a home and a career, for both of which she was inordinately grateful. Professionally, her life was fulfilling. Socially too she kept busy. She went to the theatre and the cinema, with Natasha and other friends. And as her circle of acquaintance had widened she'd begun to attend dinner parties. She smiled and chatted to the pleasant men who'd been invited to partner her, and, watched with wistful anxiety by her hostesses, politely evaded the inevitable follow-up invitations.

There would come a time when her personal life would need fulfilment again; she was sure of it. But that time was not yet. At present, celibacy seemed much the safer option.

And right now she had another choice to make. Should she stay, or should she run? Her primary instinct told her to get out, and fast. She had suffered enough already at Ross's hands.

But reason advised caution. Maybe this meeting, so long dreaded, was the very catalyst she needed in order to close the lid on the past once and for all. Achieve some kind of closure on a relationship that should never have existed in the first place.

And there were other factors to take into account—Christy's disappointment at losing her matron of honour not being the least. It would be selfish and unkind to upset arrangements that had been months in the planning. And it was improbable that anyone else could possibly wear the slender sheath of primrose silk that she planned to wear as she followed Christy up the aisle.

Besides—and this was important too—Ross would doubtless be expecting her to vanish back to London—to take the coward's way out, she thought, her mouth twisting. And why should she oblige him by being so predictable?

Far better to let him see how little she cared about the past by standing her ground and toughing it out.

After all, it was only three days to the wedding, and then she could quite legitimately return to London—although she knew her aunt and uncle had been hoping she might stay on for a few days.

I, she thought, can survive three days.

'Jenna.'

Over the boom of the surf, and the mourning of the wind, she heard her name spoken.

For a moment she was very still, telling herself with a kind of desperation that it couldn't be true. That it was just a figment of her imagination, conjured up because she had allowed herself to think about Ross—to indulge memories that were best ignored.

'Jenna.'

She heard it again, and knew there could be no mistake—and no respite either. The moment she had feared all these months was upon her at last.

Because no one else had ever said her name with quite that same intonation, the first syllable softened and deliberately emphasised.

There was a time when that sound alone had had the power to melt her bones, as if she felt the touch of his hand, the brush of his lips on her naked skin.

Now it seemed as if a stone had lodged, hard and cold, in the pit of her stomach. Her hands tightened briefly, convulsively, on the back of the bench, and the roar of the sea was no louder than the thunder of her own pulses as slowly she turned to face him.

He was, she discovered, startled, only a few yards away from her. How could she not have known—not been aware of his approach? Her emotional antennae must have been dulled by all those false alarms in the past.

Striving for composure, she balled her hands into fists and thrust them deep into the pockets of her jacket. If they were going to start shaking it was no one's business but her own, she thought, and she made herself meet his gaze.

Although it was not easy to do so. His eyes went over her, slowly, searchingly, the straight black brows drawing together in a slight frown.

She knew exactly what he was seeing. The brown suede covered a tawny jersey. A silk scarf was knotted at her throat, and her long legs were booted to the knee under a brief skirt in pale tweed.

A successful, even affluent look—casual, but confident.

And she needed every scrap of confidence that was at her disposal.

He, she saw, was wearing black. Close-fitting pants that stressed the length of his legs, a roll-neck sweater and a leather jacket.

Belated mourning? she wondered bitterly, as the block of stone inside her twisted slowly. Agonisingly.

He said abruptly, 'You're thinner.'

It was so totally typical of him, Jenna thought, almost stung to unexpected laughter. None of the niceties or formalities of polite conversation for Ross. No cautious breaking of the ice between two people who had parted badly and never met since.

Well, if that was how he wanted to play it...

She shrugged. 'Then I'm in fashion.' She kept her tone cool to the point of indifference.

He smiled, that familiar, ironic twist of the mouth. 'Since when did you care about that?'

'Perhaps I've changed,' she said. 'People do.'

He shook his head slowly, his eyes never leaving hers. 'You haven't changed so much,' he said. 'Or how would I have known where to find you?' He gestured towards the sea. 'This was always your favourite place.'

'You came—looking for me?' She could not suppress the note of incredulity, but managed a tiny laugh to cover it. 'And I thought it was just a ghastly coincidence.'

'I thought perhaps we should—talk a little.'

'I really don't think we have anything left to talk about,' Jenna told him crisply. 'Our lawyers said all that was necessary quite some time ago.'

'However, they're not here,' he said softly. 'But we are. And that's the problem.'

'Is there a problem? I didn't realise...'

He sighed. 'Jenna—do you want to play games or talk sense?' He paused questioningly, and when she did not reply went on, 'Can we at least agree that this isn't a situation either of us would have chosen?'

'Your stepmother clearly thinks differently.'

'Thirza is a genuinely kind woman,' he said. 'But sometimes her kindness leads her in strange directions.' He shrugged. 'What can I say?' He was silent again for a moment. 'Please believe that she didn't see fit to mention to me that Christy was to be married at this time—or that you would be attending the wedding. Otherwise I would not be here.'

'Well,' Jenna said, trying for crisp lightness, 'no one told me about you either. You'd almost think they were playing a late April Fool on us.'

'And I think, unless we are careful, we could both end up looking like fools,' Ross returned tersely. 'So, if you're thinking of doing a runner back to London, I advise you to forget it.'

Jenna gasped. 'May I remind you that you no longer have the right to dictate my actions?'

He said gently, 'And may I remind you that it was never a right I chose to enforce, anyway?'

She bit her lip. 'You realise the local gossips will have a field-day if we both stay.'

'They will have even more to enjoy if we leave.'

'Why?'

'Because they will think it means that we still matter to each other—when we know that's not the case.'

'On that,' she said, her tone gritty, 'we can agree, at least.'

'Good,' he said. 'We're making progress.' He paused. 'Unfortunately, it will be equally harmful if we each pretend the other does not exist—and for the same reason.'

'Ye-es,' she acknowledged, slowly and reluctantly. 'I suppose so.'

'Then I suggest that for the duration of the wedding celebrations we maintain a pretence of civility with each other.' He spoke briskly. 'Not for my sake, of course, or even yours, but for Christy.' He paused. 'I don't want her big day to be marred by the spectacle of us making ourselves ridiculous—or an object of speculation for the whole community, either,' he added grimly. 'I'm sure that's a point of view you can share.'

'How reasonable you make it sound,' Jenna said with a snap.

'Fine,' he threw back at her. 'Then go back to London. Let them think that you still care too much to be near me, even in public.'

'Now you really are being ridiculous,' she said coldly. 'As a matter of fact, I'd already made up my mind to stay. But I admit I hoped you'd have the decency to keep out of the way.'

'Decency was never one of my virtues.' His drawl taunted her. 'And I gather Thirza has already told the Penloes that I will be escorting her to the wedding. So I think we're going to have to—grin and bear it.'

'By taking refuge in clichés?'

'By doing whatever it takes.' He paused again, and she was uneasily aware of that intent, assessing stare. 'So, shall we each take a deep breath and declare a temporary truce—for the duration of the wedding?'

Jenna bit her lip. 'It seems there is no alternative.'

'Then shall we shake hands on it?' He walked towards her, closing the space between them, and she couldn't retreat because the damned bench was in the way. Could do nothing about the fact that he was now standing right beside her.

He held out his hand, his dark eyes mesmeric, compelling. Then a mischievous gust of wind suddenly lifted her loosened hair and blew it across his face.

Ross gasped and took a step backwards, his hands tearing almost feverishly at the errant strands to free himself.

For a crazy moment she wondered if he was remembering, as she was, the way he'd used to play with her hair when they were in bed together after lovemaking, twining it round his fingers and drawing it across his lips and throat.

And how she would bury her face in his shoulder, luxuriously inhaling the scent of his skin…

Sudden pain wrenched at her uncontrollably. Blood was roaring in her ears. Hands shaking, she raked her hair back from her face and held it captive at the nape of her neck.

She said hoarsely, looking past him, 'I—I think the weather's getting worse. I—I'll see you around—I expect…'

She walked away from him, forcing herself not to hurry, across the short, damp grass.

And if he said her name again as she went the wind carried it away and it was lost for ever. And she could only be thankful for that.

Once safely inside the garden she began to run, stumbling a little as her feet crunched the gravel.

She fell breathlessly through the front door and met Christy, back from her shopping trip to Truro, coming downstairs.

'Darling,' Christy's blue eyes searched her face. 'Are you all right? Ma was worried about you…'

'I'm fine,' Jenna said, eyes fiercely bright, cheeks hectically flushed. 'And, for good or ill, I'm staying. But on one condition—and it's not negotiable.'

'Oh, Jen.' Christy hugged her. 'Anything—you know that.'

Jenna took a deep, steadying breath. 'I'm going into Polcarrow tomorrow—and I'm having my hair cut.' She paused. 'All of it.'

CHAPTER TWO

THE wind dropped during the early hours of the morning. Jenna could have timed it to the minute, if she'd felt inclined, as she'd done little else since she got to bed but lie staring into the darkness and listening to the grandfather clock in the hall below sonorously marking the passage of the night.

If I don't get some sleep soon I'm going to look and feel like hell in the morning, she told herself, turning on to her stomach and giving her inoffensive pillows a vicious pummelling.

Even so, there was no way she would look as bad as Ross had done yesterday, she realised with a pang of reluctant concern. Any doubts she might have had about the seriousness of his recent illness had shattered after the first glance. Because he'd looked as if the virus he'd picked up abroad had taken him to death's door and back again.

He had told her she was thinner, but he too had lost an untold amount of weight, and his dark face had been haggard, and sallow, with deep shadows under his eyes. He'd looked older, too, and quieter. And oddly weary. For a moment she had found herself confronted by a stranger.

She could understand now why Thirza had been so worried about him, even if she did not relish the solution that worry had produced.

She sighed, burying her face in the pillow. For a while she'd been seriously tempted to keep quiet about their encounter on the cliff, but she'd soon realised that would be impractical. Besides, the way that she and Ross planned to deal with each other would have a direct bearing on the next few days, and affect her family, so they probably had a right to know.

She'd broken the news of their truce over dinner, keeping her voice light and matter-of-fact.

'The last thing either of us wants is to make the situation more awkward than it already is.' She had tried to smile. 'So, we plan to be— civil.'

There was a silence, then Aunt Grace said, 'Oh, my dear child, how desperately sad.' She directed a fulminating stare at her husband, who was placidly eating his portion of chicken casserole. 'Henry—how long have you known that Ross would be bringing Thirza to the wedding—and why on earth did you agree?'

'She rang to inform me just this morning.' Mr Penloe smiled at his wife. 'And she didn't ask my permission,' he added drily.

'Typical,' Grace Penloe said hotly. 'Absolutely *typical*. If she'd had the least consideration for us all she'd have stayed away herself.'

Jenna laid a placatory hand over her aunt's. 'Darling, it's all right—really. I admit I was upset when I first heard Ross was here, but that was—just me being silly.' She gave a resolute smile. 'It could be all for the best,' she added, with a sideways glance at her uncle. 'After all, we had to meet again some time.'

'Probably,' said Mrs Penloe. 'But, for preference, not under the Polcarrow microscope. Oh, Betty Fox will make a meal of this,' she added, stabbing at a mushroom as if it were the lady in question.

'Betty Fox will have enough to do, criticising what we're all wearing and finding fault with the decorations in the church hall and the caterers,' Christy said, pulling a face. 'Even she can't make much capital out of a divorced couple being polite to each other.'

'That's what you think,' her mother said tartly. 'Oh, damn Thirza.' She paused ominously. 'And, Jenna, what's this Christy tells me about you making an appointment at the hairdresser tomorrow to have your hair cut?'

Jenna shrugged. 'New attitude—new image. I've had long hair all my life. It's time for a change.'

Mrs Penloe gave the smooth chestnut coil at the nape of her niece's neck an anguished look. 'Oh, Jenna, don't do it. At least, not now. Wait until the wedding is over, please.'

Jenna stared at her. 'Aunt Grace, I'll be wearing a spray of freesias in my hair. The style won't make any difference.'

'I wasn't thinking of the headdress.' Mrs Penloe shook her head. 'Oh, dear.'

'You'd think,' Jenna said later, as she gave the condemned hair its final nightly brushing, 'that I was having my head cut off instead.'

Christy, who was sprawled across the bed, turning over the pages of *House and Garden*, frowned. 'Ma did overreact slightly,' she agreed. 'I can't say I'm entranced with the idea myself, but it's your hair, and your decision.'

She pulled a face. 'Perhaps th...
starting to get to her at last. She's b...
ingly calm and organised so far, un...
Thirza dropped her bombshell, that is. I'v...
Pops that when it's all over he should take ...
away for a holiday.'

A sharp gust rattled the window, and the
girls exchanged wry glances.

'Preferably somewhere warm and peaceful,'
Jenna said drily, putting down her brush.

'Thank heavens we decided to have the reception in the church hall, instead of...'
Christy paused awkwardly.

Jenna sent her a composed smile. 'Instead
of a marquee on the lawn as I did?' she queried. 'It's all right. You can mention it without
me having hysterics.' She pulled a face. 'I suspect I'll need to grow another skin over the
next few days, anyway.'

Christy shut the magazine and sat up. 'Jen—
I'm so awfully sorry you should be put through
this.' She paused. 'The village rumour mill had
Ross totally bedridden and being fed intrave-
nously, of course, so you'd hardly expect him
to pop up on Trevarne Head, being civilised.'
She gave Jenna an anxious look. 'Seeing him
again—was it as bad as you feared?'

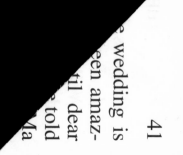

...a said lightly. *Worse—*

...ief.' Christy shook her ...Thirza off the hook. As ...eration and family unity, ...bric designer.'

...ly that, all right,' Jenna agreed. 'In fact, I've often thought I'd like to stage an exhibition of her work at the gallery.'

'You could always suggest it.'

Jenna shook her head. 'She'd refuse. I was never her favourite person, even before the divorce.'

'I could never figure that,' Christy said thoughtfully. 'After what she went through with her own husband, I'd have said her sympathies would have been with you.' She paused ruefully. 'Ouch, my big mouth again. Jen, I'm so sorry...'

'Don't be,' Jenna said briskly as she applied her moisturiser. 'Now, tell me about the best man instead. He's supposed to be my perk, isn't he?'

'Oh, Tim's adorable.' Christy cheered noticeably. 'He works in the City, too, and he and Adrian have been friends since university. They're arriving in time for lunch tomorrow.'

She lowered her voice confidentially. 'And I happen to know Tim's not seeing anyone just now.'

'Christy,' Jenna said gently, 'be content with your lovely Adrian, and don't try match-making for other people. I was thinking of having a dance with Tim—nothing more.'

'Why not have two or three dances?' Christy suggested, unperturbed. She gave a sly smile. 'He'll make excellent camouflage, if nothing else.'

'I'll think about it.' Jenna rose from the dressing table. 'Now, push off, bride, and get some beauty sleep.'

'There are still three days to go,' Christy protested as Jenna ushered her inexorably to the door.

'True, but you need all the help you can get,' she said wickedly, and closed the door, laughing, on her cousin's outrage.

Now I'm the one who needs help, she thought drily, as she turned over in bed yet again, trying to relax and failing. This insomnia is probably Christy's curse on me.

But in her heart she knew that it was not that simple. That her restlessness and unease were really due to Ross's reappearance in her life and nothing else.

Which was quite ridiculous, she told herself forcefully. Because he wouldn't be losing a moment's sleep over her, in Thirza's slate-roofed cottage on the outskirts of the village.

Once again so near, she thought, yet so far away. Which seemed to sum up the entirety of their brief marriage.

Once before, on the night before their wedding, when she hadn't been able to sleep because she was too keyed up with joy and excitement, she'd tried to work out exactly what the distance was that separated them from each other, mentally retracing her steps down the drive from Trevarne House to the lane, narrow between its high summer hedges, and down its winding length to the steep sprawl of Polcarrow, counting her paces as she went. Imagining him opening the door of the cottage to smile at her. Holding out his arms to enfold her...

Suddenly Jenna found herself sitting up, gasping for breath. She was shaking all over and her nightdress was clinging to her sweat-dampened body. She fumbled for the switch of the bedside lamp, then poured herself some

water from the carafe on the night table, gulp-
ing its coolness past the constriction in her
throat.

'Oh, you idiot,' she whispered to herself.
'You pathetic fool.'

The phrase 'don't even go there' had never
seemed more appropriate, yet she almost had.
She'd created a trap for herself and nearly
fallen into it. Because she couldn't afford these
memories. They brought too much pain with
them.

The ending of her marriage had been a war
zone, and she still bore the wounds. And this
truce that she'd agreed on with Ross was
meaningless, because it would never lead to a
lasting peace.

That was impossible, she thought. Too much
had happened.

Most of it she'd managed to block out over
the past months by working hard and making
sure her leisure hours were full, leaving little
time for introspection. But now there was a
crack in the dam, and she was terrified of what
might follow.

She switched off the lamp and lay down
again, aware that her stomach was churning
and a mass of confused thoughts were jostling

for precedence in her tired mind. And, with them, memories as sharp as knives.

Memories that she needed to deal with and forget. As Ross himself, no doubt, had done long ago.

And that, she realised unhappily, was no comfort at all.

'Are you sure about this?' said Stella, picking up a length of Jenna's hair and brandishing it.

She was short, wiry and feisty, with hair that—this week—was the colour of pewter. She was an 'incomer' too—someone who'd come to Cornwall on holiday and fallen in love with it, then decided to throw up her job in a top London hairdressing salon and make a new life for herself in Polcarrow.

She'd lost no time in opening her own premises in the village's steep main street, and her skills had attracted clients from all over the Duchy.

On Saturday she would be bringing two assistants and a friend who was a beautician and manicurist to Trevarne House to attend to the needs of the bride and her family.

In the meantime she'd agreed to squeeze in an appointment for Jenna. But she clearly wasn't happy about it.

'What happens if I start and you change your mind?' she demanded pugnaciously, hands on hips. 'I can't stick it back on, you know.' Her tone changed, became wheedling. 'Why don't I just give it a good trim instead?'

'I'm quite serious.' Jenna said flatly. 'I want it short.' She opened the style book and pointed. 'Like that.'

'Hell's bells,' said Stella, blinking. 'All right, then, love. But it's your funeral.'

Three quarters of an hour later, Jenna found herself regarding a stranger in the mirror. Her chestnut mane had been reduced to little more than a sleek cap, skilfully layered, which emphasised the shape of her head and lay in feathered fronds across her forehead and over her ears.

'Actually, it works,' Stella conceded unwillingly. 'It shows off your cheekbones and that. And on Saturday I can fix your flowers—like this.' She demonstrated.

Jenna smiled at her. 'Stella—you're a genius.'

'Yeah,' said Stella, who did not count mock-modesty as a virtue. 'But I still say it's a shame. All that lovely hair.' She paused. 'Want a bit to keep? Reminder of past glories, eh?'

'No,' Jenna said quietly. 'I don't think so, thanks.'

Her head felt incredibly light as she emerged into the street, and the sun had come out too—doubtless in honour of her new image.

She had parked her car down by the harbour, and progress back to it was slow. Every few yards, it seemed, people were stopping her to welcome her back, to tell her she looked wonderful, and say that it looked as if the weather might clear up after all for the wedding.

And she smiled back, and thanked them and agreed, saying she would see them on Saturday.

Amid the general euphoria of welcome it took a moment to register that she was being watched with less than warmth from across the street. She glanced up and saw that Ross was standing on the narrow pavement, outside Betty Fox's general stores. He was still to the point of tension, staring at her, his brows drawn together in thunderous incredulity.

Jenna's instinct was to make a dash for the car, but instead she made herself smile weakly and lift her hand in a half-greeting.

He moved then, crossing the street, weaving his way between two vans and a bicycle with the long, lithe stride that was so hauntingly familiar.

What a difference a few hours could make, Jenna thought in astonishment as he reached her. Yesterday on the cliff he had looked tired, almost defeated. Today he was clearly incandescent, and her heart began to thud in alarm.

His hand closed, not gently, on her arm. 'In the name of God,' he grated, 'what have you done to yourself?'

'I've had my hair cut.' She tried unavailingly to free herself from his grasp. 'It's not a crime.'

'That,' Ross said crushingly, 'is a matter of opinion.'

'And, anyway,' Jenna went on, her own anger sparking into life, 'it's none of your damned business what I do.'

'So, if I see an act of vandalism being committed—a work of art being defaced—I'm to say or do nothing? Or should I stand back and applaud?'

'Don't be ridiculous,' she snapped. 'It's not the same thing at all, and you know it.'

'No,' he said. 'It's far worse. It's a travesty—a sacrilege.' His eyes held hers. The noise around them—the hum of voices, the stutter of traffic, and the crying of gulls from the harbour—seemed to fade, enclosing them in a strange and potent silence.

Then, over his shoulder, Jenna saw Betty Fox emerge from her shop, ostensibly to rearrange the newspapers in the outside rack, her glance darting avidly towards them, and the spell was sharply broken.

She said tautly, 'I thought we had a truce. Yet here we are brawling in public, for all the world to see. Now, will you kindly let go of me?'

'No,' he said. 'Not yet.'

He set off down the street, still holding her arm, taking Jenna with him whether she wanted to go or not, turning the corner on to the harbour.

'What the hell do you think you're doing.' She was flushed, breathless with indignation at being whirled along in this undignified manner.

He had always done this, she thought. Starting with that night in London when they'd met again. Recognised each other in a totally new way...

'Come.' He'd taken her arm then, hurrying her from the room—from the building and into the street. Striding so fast that she'd had to run to keep up with him.

'Where are we going?' She'd been overwhelmed by all she felt for him—scared, joyous and hungry all at the same time.

And he'd stopped suddenly, and turned to her, his hands framing her face with heart-stopping tenderness. 'Does it matter?'

Now, even though there was nothing remotely lover-like in his touch, she was shocked to find it could still shake her to the core. Or was that the memory it evoked?

'Making amends, darling,' he flung back at her. 'Being amazingly civilised.'

He pushed open the door of the Quayside Café and marched her in. For a startled moment the buzz of conversation at the occupied tables faltered, then resumed at a slightly higher pitch as Ross ushered Jenna to a table beside the window and ordered two coffees from the flustered proprietress.

'Would you like something to eat?' he asked Jenna, glancing towards the counter laden with cakes, biscuits and scones.

'Thank you, no,' she returned glacially.

His face relaxed into a sudden grin. 'Because it would choke you?'

It did not help her temper to know she'd actually been tempted, just for a moment, to smile back. 'This is all a big joke to you, isn't it?' she said in a furious undertone.

His brows lifted. 'Far from it, sweetheart,' he drawled. 'A tragedy, perhaps.' He paused. 'Now, perhaps we should find some bland neutral topic to keep us from each other's throats until the coffee comes.'

'You think of something,' she said curtly. 'I'm not into small talk.'

'Fine.' He thought for a moment. 'Are you planning to go on holiday this year?'

'I haven't decided yet.' She looked down at the checked tablecloth. 'I might go for a last-minute booking on some Greek island.'

'Alone?'

She shrugged. 'I can hardly go with Natasha. One of us has to be there to run the gallery.'

'Yes, of course,' he said softly. 'Thirza told me that you were now in business together.'

There was a note in his voice that reminded her that Natasha's low opinion of him had been entirely reciprocated.

She lifted her chin. 'How kind of your step-mother to take such an interest in my affairs.'

'A slight exaggeration.' The dark eyes glinted. 'She merely mentioned it in passing.'

'I see.' She hesitated. 'What about you? Are you—planning any kind of vacation?'

He smiled faintly. 'For me, as ever, a holi-day is simply to stop travelling.'

But you did stop—when you married me. You said you'd finished with that kind of life. The thought forced itself upon her before she could prevent it.

'But I suppose I'll go back to the house in Brittany,' he went on. 'Apparently the last lot of tenants weren't the most careful in the world, and it needs some work.'

'You've been renting out Les Roches?' *The place where we spent our honeymoon?* 'I—I didn't know.'

Ross shrugged. 'Houses shouldn't be left empty, or the heart goes out of them.'

Jenna examined a fleck on her thumbnail. 'You've never considered selling it?'

'No.' The response was crisp and instant. 'It's always been a family home.' He leaned back in his chair. 'And one day I intend to have a family there.'

She had not seen that coming, and she felt as if she'd been punched in the solar plexus. There was an odd roaring in her ears, and when she parted her lips to say something— anything—no sound would come.

The arrival of the coffee saved her. By the time the cups had been placed on the table, and cream and sugar brought, she was able to speak again. To cover, she hoped, the momentary hiatus.

'My God.' She even managed a little laugh. 'Is the rolling stone coming to rest at last?'

'It would seem so.' His mouth twisted. 'As they all do—eventually.'

'I thought you might prove to be the exception.' She could only hope the lightness in her tone was convincing. 'What's caused the change of heart?'

'I became ill.' His gaze met hers. 'And, as you know, I'm not used to that. It made me think. Perhaps—adjust my priorities.' He was silent for a moment, then he said, 'Also, there is—someone in my life. Someone important.' He shrugged. 'What can I say?'

'There's nothing that needs to be said.' Stunned as she was, somehow she found the words. Made her lips utter them without faltering. 'After all, we're both—free agents. When—when's the happy day?'

'Nothing's been decided yet. It is still a little too soon for her. She's been married before as well, and there are adjustments to be made.'

'Well,' she said, smiling resolutely, 'naturally you'll want to be sure—this time.'

'Yes,' he said. 'I will.' His brows lifted. 'You're—very understanding.'

She murmured something and looked down at the table. The compliment was undeserved, and she knew it. She understood nothing. Under her façade of composure she was seething with questions that she would not—could not ask him.

Do I know her? being the foremost. To be followed by, *Is it Lisa Weston? And, if not, why not? What happened to the woman for whom you ended our marriage?* And, *Did you tire of her, too, in the end?* The words were tumbling over themselves in her mind, demanding answers.

But these were places she dared not go. Because once the questions started she might not be able to stop them.

And the inner ice she relied on might crack, and all the pain—all the loss—might come pouring out at last. Betraying her utterly.

Revealing to him, once and for all, how deeply he had wounded her.

And revealing, most damagingly of all, that she still bled—still grieved in spite of the two years' total separation between them.

And if he ever suspected the healing process in her had not begun, he might ask himself why. And she could not risk that particular humiliation, she thought breathlessly, or any other.

Aware that the silence between them was lengthening, she looked up and smiled brightly at him across the table.

His own glance was hooded, meditative. 'And what about you, Jenna? Is there someone for you?'

'No one that special.' She lifted a nonchalant shoulder. 'But I'm enjoying playing the field. I never really did that before.'

'No,' he said. He drank some coffee, grimaced and put down his cup. 'This place serves the worst coffee in the world.'

'You've said that every time we've been here.' The words were out before she could stop them. They were loaded with shared memory. And just when she needed to make him think the past was a closed book, she thought, biting her lip.

'That could be because it's always true.' He glanced at his watch. 'Maybe it's time to bring our demonstration of ex-marital harmony to an end.'

'Yes—yes, of course.' She made a business of picking up her bag, watching from under her lashes as he walked to the counter to pay the bill, smiling at plump Mrs Trewin and saying something that made her bridle girlishly.

But that was Ross, she told herself stonily. He could use charm like a weapon, and it was something to which his new lady would have to accustom herself.

However, she couldn't get over the astonishing change just a few hours had wrought in him.

He looked, she thought wonderingly, as if he'd woken, refreshed, from a deep sleep. He was still too thin, of course, but the lines of his face looked sharper, more dynamic this morning, and the old glint was back in his eyes—sexy, humorous, and as devastating as ever.

Perhaps he was looking for closure, too, wanting to go into his new relationship without baggage from the past to slow him down.

And that, of course, was what she should be seeking, too. Had always told herself that she was striving to attain.

Christy's wedding was supposed to be a step on the path to her own regeneration. She had known ever since she received the invitation that she would have to be strong to cope with all the implications and resonances of the occasion. But that had been before the bombshell of Ross's presence had been exploded, and all that had happened since.

Culminating in the revelations of the past half-hour.

And now, she knew, she was going to need every single weapon in her armoury of self-protection to get her unscathed through the next few days, let alone the eternity to come. And she was frightened.

She walked ahead of him out on to the cobbles, and stood for a moment, shading her eyes, looking at the familiar mix of fishing boats and sailing craft in the harbour, thankful to have something else to focus on.

Ross came to stand beside her. 'You must miss this place—the sea—very much. Do you think you will ever come back?'

'It was a wonderful place to spend my childhood.' She kept her voice steady. 'But I'm grown-up now, and my life is—elsewhere.'

'London?' His mouth twisted. 'Even when we lived there together I was never convinced it was the right place for you.'

'Perhaps it wasn't the environment,' she said tautly, 'but other factors that were wrong. Anyway, I'd prefer not to discuss it.' She squared her shoulders. 'My car's over there. Do you want a lift back to Thirza's?'

He said slowly. 'That would be kind. But are you sure you wish to do this?'

She didn't look at him. 'We may as well keep the charade going to the bitter end.'

There was still a breeze, but it was turning into a perfect spring day. The clouds were high and broken, and the sun was hot and bright on Jenna's newly shorn head as they walked along the quayside. She slipped off the quilted gilet she was wearing and pushed up the sleeves of her thin wool sweater.

He said suddenly, his voice faintly hoarse, 'Dear God—did I do that?'

Glancing down, Jenna saw the red marks, clearly visible on her bare arm, where his fingers had gripped her.

She said, 'It's—not important. And the dress I'm wearing for the wedding has long sleeves. Besides,' she added, coolly and pointedly. 'I always did bruise easily.'

His swift smile was humourless. 'Ah, yes. Of course. How could I forget? Whereas I, on the other hand, remained unmarked and untouched by everything—always. As if I have chain mail instead of skin. Is that what you're saying?'

She bit her lip. 'Not exactly. I—I couldn't expect you to care about—some things in the same way as I did.'

'Presumably because I am an insensitive boor of a man, who understands nothing of a woman's innermost feelings.' His tone was suddenly icy. 'You have a short memory, Jenna. In those first few months of our marriage I came to know all your most intimate secrets—including some you'd never been aware of yourself until then.'

Her suddenly flushed cheeks owed nothing to the heat of the day.

She said in a suffocated voice, 'You have no right to talk to me like this. No right at all.'

'I need no reminder,' Ross said softly, 'of all the rights in you that I was fool enough to surrender.'

His words seemed to hang in the air between them, challenging, even threatening. Reviving old memories—old hungers. Shocking her with their potency.

He was watching her, the dark eyes glittering as they travelled over her in unashamed exploration. The cream round-necked sweater and close-fitting blue denim jeans she wore were no barrier to the intensity of his scrutiny, she realised as she stared back at him, eyes dilating, lips parted. Aware of a small, unwelcome stir of excitement deep within her.

Because he knew—none better—how she looked naked, after all the times he'd removed her clothes, his hands sometimes tender, often fiercely urgent. His lips caressing the warm skin he'd uncovered.

She was horrified to feel her nipples hardening involuntarily under the sudden force of the recollection.

This was what she'd always feared, she thought, swallowing. This was why she'd refused to allow any personal contact between them during the divorce, even in the safety of the lawyers' offices. Or afterwards.

Because she knew she could not guarantee to control her physical responses to him.

However much she might have trained her mind to reject him, her body still shivered with remembered desire in his presence.

Suddenly she felt heat blaze from him like a dark sun.

And realised with swift, scared certainty that all she needed to do was reach out her hand…

Her throat tightened. She thought, 'I can't do this.' And only realised she had spoken aloud when she saw his face change. The firm mouth harden.

Saw him take a step backwards, deliberately distancing himself from her.

He said quietly, 'Unfortunately, you don't have a choice, Jenna. And neither do I.' He paused. 'However, it might be better for me to walk back to Thirza's. I'll see you later.'

He turned and strode off down the quay.

For a moment Jenna stood where she was, watching him go, then, slowly and shakily, she made her way across the cobbles to her car.

She unlocked it and got in, stowing her bag on the passenger seat. Even fitting the key in the ignition. But she made no attempt to start the engine.

Her heart was thumping rapidly and noisily, and she felt slightly sick. Certainly she didn't trust herself to drive. Not unless she wanted to find herself, and the car, on the bottom of the harbour.

She thought, I have to pull myself together.

But that, of course, was easier said than done.

She drew a deep breath and made herself review the situation. It had been lousy luck running into Ross two days in a row, but she'd make sure it didn't happen again.

She was bound to see him at the wedding, of course, but there would be plenty of other people around, and he would be easier to dodge in a crowd. And there would be the unknown Tim to act as safeguard, anyway.

Apart from the wedding rehearsal tomorrow, there was no need for her to leave Trevarne House at all, and she would make sure that her every waking moment was full—even if all she could find to do was soothing Aunt Grace.

She folded her arms on the steering wheel and leaned her forehead against them, feeling the prickle of tears against her closed eyelids.

But who, she thought, with sudden desolation, is going to soothe me?

And for that she could find no satisfactory answer at all.

CHAPTER THREE

THE car was a cocoon. A refuge closing her away from everything except her thoughts. Those she could not escape, or even evade. Not any more.

Her mind was in chaos, yet somehow she found she was being dragged inexorably back in time to that night over three years ago when she, a child no longer, had met Ross again.

There'd been a private view at the Haville Gallery for a talented young painter having his first exhibition. The evening had gone well, and a number of pictures had displayed the red dot of success. People had begun to drift away when, suddenly alerted by an odd tingle in her senses that she was being watched, Jenna had turned and seen Ross standing a few yards away, his eyes narrowed in a kind of stunned disbelief as he looked at her.

They might have been alone. None of the chattering groups around them had seemed to exist any longer.

All the breath seemed to leave her body in one deep, startled gasp as her gaze had locked with his. Read what he was thinking as if he had shouted it aloud. The total astonishing certainty of the moment had taken her a willing, helpless prisoner. Joined them both in a new and devastating recognition.

It had been as if some lifelong search was suddenly over, and the hidden treasure—the Holy Grail—was there waiting for her.

Her stomach had churned—her pulses had gone crazy. A delicious heat had spread through her veins, and her senses had gone spinning into a kind of delirium.

And then she'd seen him smile and start towards her, and she had moved, too, going to meet him halfway. More than halfway. People had spoken to her, but she hadn't heard what they said. She'd been oblivious, every fibre of her being focussed on this man now re-entering her life with such unbelievable impact. She'd realised that she was accepting without question that here was the only man in the world whom she would ever want.

And that it was how, in some strange unfathomable way, she had always known it would be.

When she'd reached him, her voice had been a little husky croak. 'What are you doing here?'

'I was invited. Someone I met at a party.' She watched him draw an uneven breath. 'I—I almost didn't come…'

And they both laughed in derisive rejection of the very idea. Because they knew that since time began it had been inevitable that they would meet again at this place—at this moment. That this was what they had both been created for, and that there was nothing that could have kept them apart.

She said, her voice smiling, 'You recognised me—in this crowd?'

He said slowly, 'I'd have known you anywhere.' He paused. 'But why are you here?'

'It's where I work.'

'Of course.' He shook his head. 'Thirza told me that you'd done an art course.'

'I'm surprised she remembered.'

He said quietly, 'But I asked about you, Jenna. I always—always asked about you.'

And as she met his eyes, and saw the flare of passion, the unhidden hunger, she felt her skin warm passionately and involuntarily, and her throat tighten in a sweet excitement she had never known before.

She said, in a whisper, 'I—I don't understand. What is happening?'

'We are.' His voice was almost harsh. 'We're happening to each other. At long last.' His hand touched her cheek, stroked its curve, and she turned her head in a swift, involuntary reaction, finding his caressing fingers with her lips.

'Jenna.' He spoke in a tortured whisper. 'Dear God, Jenna...'

For a moment he was silent, mastering his breathing. Then, 'Come.' He took her arm, hurrying her from the room—from the building and into the street. Striding so fast that she had to run to keep up with him.

'I can't just leave...' But her protest carried no real conviction.

'You just did.'

'Where are we going?' She was overwhelmed by all she felt for him—scared, joyous and hungry all at the same time.

And he stopped suddenly and turned to her, his hands framing her face with heart-stopping tenderness. 'Does it matter?'

And she replied simply and seriously, 'No.'

They went to his flat in a warehouse development overlooking the Thames. As he sat beside her in the shadowed intimacy of the taxi Ross took her hand and held it. There was no real pressure in the clasp of his fingers, but his touch seemed to penetrate to her bones, and she began to tremble inside.

Yet as they rode in the lift to the upper floor Jenna found her first euphoria evaporating, leaving her feeling shy and vulnerable. She cast a swift, sideways glance at Ross, but there was nothing to be read from his expression. Suddenly he seemed to be the cool, enigmatic stranger of her teens again, and she was assailed by a pang of real doubt.

What am I doing? she thought. Why am I here?

Well, she knew the answer to that, of course. She might be inexperienced, but she wasn't naïve. And she had gone with him of her own free will, so she could hardly protest if he expected her to keep the promise that her capitulation implied, she thought, swallowing.

But her first glimpse inside the flat itself drove everything else from her mind. Eyes widening, she stared round at the high vaulted ceilings and enormous windows which provided untrammelled views of the river from the main living area. The wooden floors gleamed with the patina of gold, and the pale walls provided a neutral background for furnishings and drapes in warm earth colours.

'I bought the shell,' Ross told her, as he began to make coffee in the streamlined galley kitchen. 'Then I got a mate of mine who's an architect to design the interior, because I needed space for an office and a dark room.'

'He's made a wonderful job of it.' Jenna's eyes shone as she looked around her. 'It's amazing.'

He grinned at her. 'And that's even before you get the guided tour.' He paused. 'Have you had anything to eat this evening—apart from those little bits of nothing on toast?'

'I'm glad Mr Haville can't hear you,' Jenna told him with severity. 'Those were canapés from very expensive caterers.'

'Which could explain the fashionable minimalistic effect. And also why I'm starving.' Ross briskly abandoned coffee-making and produced a pack of dried pasta from a cupboard instead, rummaging in the fridge for eggs, pancetta and a carton of cream. 'Spaghetti carbonara?'

'Yes, please.' Jenna nodded vigorously. 'Can I help?'

'There's some rocket and stuff in the salad drawer. You could make a dressing for that.' He pointed. 'You'll find what you need in that cupboard.'

They worked for a few minutes in a silence that managed, incredibly, to be relaxed and companionable. As if, Jenna thought wonderingly, they'd been doing it all their lives...

And she was frankly relieved to find that he had no intention of dragging her into bed immediately. Because, however much her body might be clamouring for him, her first physical surrender was going to be a tremendous mental and emotional hurdle for her.

But I'll deal with that when I have to, she told herself.

As she tossed the salad leaves in a bowl, she said, 'I still can't believe this is happening.'

'You're on some strange diet that forbids evening meals?'

'I mean that we're here—like this.' She shook her head in bewilderment. 'Yet really we're practically strangers.'

'You and I have always known each other.' Ross rinsed his hands and dried them on a towel. 'And I don't mean the fact that we're probably fourth or fifth cousins by marriage. There was an awareness there from the first.' He paused. 'I think you sensed it, too.'

She blushed a little. 'Even when I was being a brat?'

His face was solemn, but his eyes were dancing. 'Particularly then.'

'But—you always ignored me.'

'Have a heart, my love.' His tone was gentle. 'You were still a child. I had to keep my distance for all kinds of reasons. You must know that. Your uncle Henry certainly did,' he added drily. 'He was very kind about it. Told me I had nothing to be ashamed of. Congratulated me on identifying a potential problem and dealing with it before it became serious. Said that young girls had no idea of their own power, but enjoyed testing it anyway. That I'd been very patient and must continue to be so.'

She said in a stifled voice, 'You talked about me—like that? As if I was some junior tease? Oh, God…'

He shook his head. 'No, darling. Because we both loved you. Besides, he was quite right. I'd been shaken at the depth of my own feelings. And I couldn't explain to him that it wasn't just a physical thing. That what drew you to me was that sense of inner calm you already possessed. Christy was the open, flirty one. But you had a quality of stillness that was like a magnet to my type of vagabond. So the only answer was to go away, and stay away until you were older.'

She bent her head. 'Ross, I grew up a long time ago. But, even so, you—stayed away.'

'Yes,' he said slowly. 'Because over the years it all began to seem like an illusion. One of those private dreams that you keep locked away, because you know it can never be fulfilled.'

He paused. 'It occurred to me too that it could all be completely one-sided. That the strange feeling of attunement—of coming home—that I'd sensed had just been a figment of my imagination.'

She said huskily, 'You knew better than that.'

'Perhaps—but life moves on, and I could have missed my moment. You might easily have met someone else.' He shook his head. 'Each time I saw Thirza I was half expecting her to tell me that you were engaged or married.'

'No,' she said. 'There's never been anyone—anyone serious, that is.'

And her heart cried, *Because I was waiting for you—only I didn't realise it. I only knew when I saw you again tonight.*

He was silent for a moment, the dark eyes quizzical as he studied her.

Then he said quietly, 'I see.' And continued with his preparations for supper.

And she knew that it was true. That he recognised her longing, and her fear, and understood them both. And tonight would be a new beginning.

There was warm ciabatta bread with the food, and a dry, crisp white wine which cut across the melting richness of the pasta. And afterwards there was cheese, and a platter of fresh fruit.

In spite of the nervous flutters in the pit of her stomach, Jenna managed to eat a perfectly reasonable meal. It was partly a matter of pride. She needed to prove to herself as well as Ross that she possessed at least a modicum of sophistication, even though she might be embarking on uncharted waters.

The conversation helped reduce tension, too. They chatted easily, filling in the gaps in the years they'd been apart.

However, she was bewildered by the fact that he made no attempt to touch her at all. Indeed, in the kitchen, during the final preparations for the meal, he seemed to have gone out of his way to avoid physical contact.

Perhaps his realisation that she was still a virgin was an unwelcome one, Jenna thought unhappily. Maybe he needed someone who could meet him at his own level of experience.

Even when dinner was over, and they took their coffee and brandies with tacit consent to one of the enormous sofas, they occupied opposite corners, several feet apart.

Surely, Jenna thought, biting her lip, he couldn't be waiting for her to make the first move.

Whatever the reason, Ross seemed quite happy to go on chatting, exchanging reminiscences, and Jenna found herself catching her breath as he described, almost laconically, some of the adventures and dangers his chosen career had involved.

'I feel as if I've been living on a different planet,' she said ruefully, curled up tautly amongst the deep cushions, her feet tucked under her. She ticked off on her fingers. 'Home, school, college, job. A very sedate progression. Not much excitement there.'

'Is that what you want—excitement?' There was a smile in his voice. He was leaning back, totally at ease and sexy with it, tie loosened and the top buttons of his shirt undone, its cuffs turned back over tanned forearms.

'I don't know.' She swallowed past a sudden tightness in her throat as she realised the mood of the evening had shifted. 'I never thought about it before.'

'And now?'

'I'm still—not sure.' She shook her head, punching a clenched fist into the arm of the sofa. 'Oh, how feeble does that sound?'

He said quietly, 'Darling, there's no need for you to beat yourself up over this, I promise you.' He paused. 'Or to be scared, either.'

'I—I'm not...'

'No?' His eyes were quizzical. 'You're so brittle that if I laid a hand on you, you'd probably shatter into a million pieces.'

She lifted her chin, meeting his gaze. 'Maybe I'm tougher than I look. And I have been touched before,' she added for good measure.

'Really?' The dark eyes studied her, lingering with sensuous candour on the curve of her breasts, then travelled slowly down to the slender outline of her thighs under the cling of her simple black dress. 'Would you care to specify how—and where?'

She said, 'You're laughing at me...'

'I promise I was never more serious.' There was a sudden harshness in his voice. 'Make no mistake, I want you very badly, Jenna. I need you to stay with me tonight, but I won't force you into something you're not ready for.'

He took a deep breath. 'If it's all too soon, and too sudden for you, then you only have to say so. It's not a problem. I have the number of a reliable cab company to take you home.'

She said with difficulty, 'And then?'

He shrugged wryly. 'Then I practise superhuman patience—and wait.'

'But for how long?'

His mouth tightened. 'You want your pound of flesh, don't you? Very well. The answer is for as long as it takes—but no further than our wedding night,' he added drily. 'Because then I might have to insist.'

She stared at him. 'You—want to—marry me?'

He moved then. Closer, but still not crowding her. Reached out a hand and took a long strand of hair, winding it round his fingers.

He said quietly, staring down at its glossy sheen, 'You surely can't think that, having found you, I'm ever going to let you go again?'

Her heart was pounding like a beaten drum.

'Isn't it usual to make some kind of formal proposal?'

His grin was rueful. 'I planned to—in the morning.'

'Oh,' she said slowly. Then 'May I use your phone?'

'Of course.' He released her immediately. 'You'll find the card for a minicab tucked inside the directory.'

Jenna shook her head. 'I'm calling my flatmate—to tell her I won't be back tonight.' She smiled rather waveringly. 'You see, I really don't do this, and she may—worry.'

'Darling.' He slipped off the sofa and knelt in front of her. His voice was very gentle. 'Are you sure about this?'

'Yes,' she said. 'I am now. I'm quite certain that if I'm going to spend the rest of my life with you I'd like it to begin tonight.'

Ross bent his head and rested his cheek for a long moment against her stockinged knee. He said softly, 'Then so it shall.'

She got the answering machine when she called the flat. Perhaps Natasha was already in bed, she thought, glancing at her watch. Or, worse, still at the gallery, helping to clear up after the private view.

But no amount of guilt could hide the note of lilting joy in her voice. 'Hi. This is to let you know that I'm fine—and I'll see you in the morning.'

Then she replaced the handset and, smiling, her heart in her eyes, walked sweetly and simply into Ross's waiting arms.

God, but he'd made it so easy for her, Jenna thought wearily, remembering. But then he'd hardly had to try.

It had been the kind of seduction that dreams were made of. A long, sweet ascent to pleasure which had made the blood sing in her veins.

From the moment his mouth had touched hers, parting her lips in unquestioned mastery, she'd been lost, drowning in sensations she'd never guessed could exist.

She'd yielded herself totally to his kisses, returning them with eager abandonment, her whole body shivering with delight as he'd lifted her into his arms and carried her to his bed.

Any last traces of shyness, any lingering doubt had been superseded entirely by a burning, overwhelming hunger which had demanded a surcease that only he could give.

She had not even questioned the practised fingers that slid off her clothes, uncovering her body in the lamplight for the arousing beguilement of his hands and lips. Nor wondered, as she'd come to do later, how many other women had moaned their longing under his smiling mouth, or arched in trembling greed for his caress.

Then, she had been blind and deaf to everything but the need to take, and be taken.

His hands had been warm as they'd explored the satin of her skin, paying a leisurely homage to every slender curve, every plane and angle of her body.

Through half-closed eyes she'd been aware that he was watching her, his own gaze intent on the play of colour under her pale skin, the drawn breath that had become a sob, the restless movement of her head on the pillow—all the small sighing answers of her body to his caresses.

She had given herself up to him with total ardour, whimpering her pleasure into his shoulder as he'd stroked and kissed her breasts, teasing her eager nipples with his tongue so that they stood proudly erect.

Her fingers had been shaking and clumsy as she'd helped to strip off his own clothing, gasping soundlessly as she'd experienced for the first time the heated power of him, naked against her nakedness.

As she'd felt the strong, clever fingers part her thighs, and discover, slowly and exquisitely, the scalding quivering centre of her being. As he'd found the tiny hidden bud and coaxed it to vibrant life, so that everything was forgotten but the agonising, essential play of his hands.

As he had drawn her slowly through the fever and torment of desire to the ultimate pinnacle and held her there for endless moments, before sending her shuddering into the stark glory of her first climax.

The ripples of delight had still been coursing through her when he'd entered her in one swift, fluid movement.

Jenna had cried out, not in pain, but in surprise and a kind of awe, her eyes dilating as they'd looked into his.

He had said her name, softly, huskily, and begun to move, gently at first, then with increasing power. And she had responded from sheer instinct, echoing the driving rhythm of his possession, her hands clasping his sweat-dampened shoulders, her slim legs locked round his lean hips, her breathing shallow, almost startled.

And she had felt, deep within her, the same primitive, devastating pressure that she'd just experienced building again. And thought, almost with fear, No—that cannot be…

Ross must have sensed her bewilderment, her momentary hesitation. His voice had reached her almost harshly, 'Darling—don't hold back. Let it happen.'

And she gasped, her head falling back on the pillow, as sheer sensation overtook her, tearing her apart in one aching convulsion after another until she thought she might die. And somewhere in the swirling golden light that consumed her she heard Ross's groan of ecstasy as he reached his own release.

A long time later, he said, 'Now you'll have to marry me.'

She lay back, smiling, in his arms, her head pillowed on his chest. 'Shouldn't that be my line?'

He dropped a kiss on her tangled hair. 'Perhaps I'm afraid you won't say it. That you'll decide you prefer just a one-night stand.'

'No,' she said, stretching luxuriously. 'That wouldn't suit me at all. And if this is domesticity, I'm all for it.'

His voice quivered into laughter. 'I'll try to give satisfaction, ma'am.'

She turned to look up at him, lifting a hand to touch his cheek. She said in a low voice, 'Ross—I never dreamed...'

He captured her hand, carrying it to his lips. 'Nor I, my love. Nor I.'

'But that can't be altogether true.' Even in her state of blissful euphoria the voice of reason intervened. 'You must have had so many women...'

'Well, that's true,' Ross said cordially. 'It's amazing I find time to eat, let alone earn my living. In fact, there's probably a queue outside now, waiting for you to leave.'

'*Oh.*' Jenna attempted to exact retribution, only to find herself being kissed into breathlessness. When she emerged, she said with dignity, 'I meant that you actually knew what to expect.'

He said gently, 'But not with you, Jenna. I was told once that sex moves to another dimension with someone you love, and I found out tonight that it's true.' He kissed her again. 'My warm, perfect girl,' he murmured with deep content.

Later still he said, 'Do you think you could live here, or would you rather look for somewhere that's new to both of us?'

'No,' she said. 'I think I could be very happy here.' She paused. 'Of course, we might have to move once we start a family.'

'Hey.' Ross sounded slightly startled. 'There's no real hurry for that, surely? Let's have some marriage first.'

'But you do want children?'

There was a slight pause, then he said, 'Yes—eventually.'

'Then that's all right.' Jenna sighed happily. 'There's still so much we don't know about each other. It's going to be wonderful finding out.'

'There could be some nasty shocks along the way, too,' Ross suggested drily.

But Jenna only laughed. 'Not a chance,' she told him airily. 'Not a chance.'

'So,' Ross said, 'as a first step on this voyage of discovery, when are you going to move in here? Do you have much stuff to shift from your present flat?'

Jenna raised her head and stared at him. 'You mean you want me to live here—before we're married?'

His brows drew together. 'That was the plan, yes. Do you have a problem with it?'

'No, but my flatmate certainly would.' Jenna's tone was rueful. 'For one thing, she relies on me for half the rent. I couldn't possibly just abandon her. I'd need to stay until she finds someone else to take my place.'

She paused. 'Besides, I've always despised women who dump their girlfriends as soon as they fall in love. And Natasha's been good to me, ever since we started working together at the gallery.'

There was an odd silence, and Jenna realised that the arm that held her had become tense. That he was staring ahead of him, his jaw set.

He said, 'I didn't realise you shared a flat.'

'Well, yes. Most people do, if they want to live somewhere half decent.'

He shrugged. 'Perhaps. I never have.' His tone was almost abrupt.

Jenna sat up. 'Ross—you really mind about this, don't you?'

He didn't reply at once. At last he said quietly, 'Is that really so strange? I—want you with me.'

'And that's what I want, too.' She looked at him appealingly. 'But you must see that I can't let Natasha down. It wouldn't be right, especially when we work together as well.'

'No,' he said. 'I suppose not. And I should admire your loyalty.'

She said slowly, 'You—you can't be jealous, surely…?'

'Can't I?' His mouth twisted. 'Maybe this is the first of those nasty shocks I mentioned.'

'I am surprised.' She smiled at him. 'Perhaps I should be flattered.'

His own grin was wry. 'I can't even use the excuse that I'm an only child and not used to sharing, because you're one, too.'

'Oh, my willingness to share has its limits.' She bent and kissed him. 'For instance, I claim exclusive rights in you,' she added softly. 'And that's not negotiable.'

'I can't wait to sign the contract.' He drew her down to him again, with sensuous purpose. 'Even if you don't move in,' he said softly, as his lips tantalised the aching peaks of her breasts, 'I hope that you'll be able to spare me the occasional night? Or several?'

'Yes,' Jenna said. 'Oh, yes.' And then she said nothing more at all for a long time.

They'd been so happy—so totally absorbed in each other, Jenna thought, her mind wincing helplessly as she remembered.

She'd been floating on a cloud by the time she'd got back to her own flat early the following morning. Unable to think of anything but how to get through the day as quickly as possible, so that she could be with Ross again that night.

She'd let herself in quietly, almost guiltily, she recalled, and crept into her room to grab a handful of clean underwear and one of the neat shirts and skirts she wore for work.

She had showered, and washed her hair, and had been sitting in bra and briefs at her dressing table, busy with the hairdryer when she suddenly realised that Natasha had appeared in the doorway behind her.

She had turned, smiling carefully. 'Oh, hi.'

'Where did you get to last night?' Natasha's eyes were fixed on her. 'You suddenly—vanished.'

'Yes.' Jenna could feel herself blushing, and cursed under her breath.

So much for playing it cool. 'I suppose I did, and I'm sorry.' She paused. 'You did get my message?'

Natasha shrugged. 'It didn't actually say much.'

'No.' Jenna bit her lip. 'You see—I accidentally bumped into an old friend—someone I haven't seen for a very long time.'

'At the viewing?' Natasha's tone was suddenly sharp.

'Why—yes.' Jenna bit her lip. 'And, naturally, we had a lot of catching up to do,' she added rather lamely.

'Did you, indeed?' Natasha said softly, her smile glinting. 'Well, it looks from here as if it was a very successful reunion. A night to remember, in fact.'

Jenna was already deeply conscious that her face was a total betrayal, her eyes shadowed and weary with sex, her skin luminous, her mouth lushly swollen. But she had nothing to regret or be ashamed of, she told herself defiantly. It wasn't as if she'd taken a vow of celibacy. And Ross was her love as well as her lover.

Her flush deepened. 'I really didn't mean to leave you in the lurch at the gallery.'

'Only you were carried away by your feelings.' Natasha paused. 'There's no need to worry. I don't think Mr Haville even noticed.'

'It went well, didn't it—the private view?' Jenna turned eagerly to an impersonal subject. She didn't want to talk about Ross, she realised. He was her sweet secret, too new and precious to be shared, even with Natasha.

Who was shrugging. 'I guess so. We certainly sold a lot of pictures.'

'Well,' Jenna said, switching off the dryer, 'that was the whole purpose of the exercise.'

'Yes,' Natasha said slowly. 'Of course it was.' Her hands tightened the belt of her robe. 'Work beckons, so I'd better get dressed.'

At the door, she paused. 'I don't mean to carp,' she said, 'or pry. But isn't all this rather out of character for you?'

Jenna bit her lip. 'I certainly didn't plan it, if that's what you mean,' she replied stiltedly. 'In fact, I had no idea Ross was going to be there, but…'

'But your eyes met across a crowded room and that was that?' There was a faint note of derision in Natasha's even voice.

'Yes.' Jenna shook her head. 'Tasha—it was incredible.' She paused, then plunged recklessly. 'He's asked me to marry him.'

There was a silence, then Natasha said softly, 'Marriage? To someone you haven't seen for years on your own admission? Are you quite mad?'

'No,' Jenna defended, then shook her head ruefully. 'Well, maybe. I don't even know any more. But I'm quite sure that I'm in love. And I've never been so happy.'

'And all this on the strength of one night.' Natasha laughed harshly. 'This Ross must be quite a stud.'

Jenna winced away from the crudity. 'It wasn't like that.' Her voice was almost stern. 'It was beautiful—and right. As if we were the other halves of each other. And that's how Ross feels, too.'

'Oh, spare me the details, please.' Her flat-mate spoke with unwonted sharpness. 'The fact is, Jenna, that you got laid—at last. And I'm glad it was good for you. But it's hardly enough to build a future on. You'd do better to play the field—see what's out there.'

Like you do? thought Jenna. A series of encounters leading nowhere while you pretend not to care?

Aloud, she said gently, 'Tasha—that's not what I want.' She shook her head. 'Perhaps I'm a one-man woman.'

'If there is such a thing.' Natasha shrugged. 'I only hope,' she added, 'that you know what you're doing.'

'Yes.' Jenna lifted her chin. 'Of course.'

Again she was accorded that flat, glittering smile. 'Well,' Natasha said softly, 'we shall see.' And went out.

But I love him, Jenna wanted to call after her. And he loves me. And he's all that I shall ever want.

All the same, some of the shine had gone out of the morning, and she put down her brush, staring at herself in the mirror. Seeing the face of a woman she barely recognised.

She thought, with an odd sense of desolation, I need Ross—here and now—to hold me. To tell me that everything's going to be all right. Oh, I need that so badly.

But she was alone.

In retrospect, Jenna could see that had been an omen, foreshadowing a tragic chain of events that had already been set in motion.

And even if she'd realised unhappiness and betrayal awaited her, would she have had the strength to break Ross's spell and walk away?

After all, everyone had tried to talk her out of her hasty marriage—had begged her to wait—give herself a breathing space. But she'd refused to listen.

Ross had warned her himself, of course, that their life would not be plain sailing. Demonstrated that he might have a darker, more complex side. Why hadn't she believed him either—and thought again?

Because I was in love, she thought tiredly. And I thought—I believed with all my heart—

that it would be enough. That it would get us through anything life might throw at us.

Which makes me all kinds of a fool. But I'm older now, and wiser—and I'm never, ever going to make that same mistake again. And that's a promise.

CHAPTER FOUR

THE sudden rap on the side of the car brought her, startled, back to the present and stark reality. She tensed, her heart thumping, turning frightened eyes towards the window, only to see Polcarrow's one and only traffic warden mouthing at her that her parking time was up.

My God, she thought, torn between shock and relief. I've been sitting here for twenty minutes. I must be crazy.

She gave the warden a jerky nod, and started the engine. Deliberately, she chose the back road out of the village rather than the direct route which would take her past Thirza's cottage.

It might be the coward's way out, but she could not risk another confrontation with Ross. Not yet, anyway. She was feeling too raw—too vulnerable after her unwise visit to the past.

Even a fleeting glimpse of him might prove more than she could bear at the moment. Because, in spite of everything he'd done, it seemed he still had the same devastating effect on her that he'd always done.

Oh, God, she thought, her hands tightening on the wheel. That's so unfair. I don't deserve it.

It was like a micro-version of the chaos theory, she decided bitterly. But instead of a butterfly flapping its wings in the jungle a virus had stirred. And it was only her life that had been thrown into turmoil as a result.

When she reached the crossroads at the top of a hill she paused, then reluctantly took the fork which led back to Trevarne House, when every instinct was encouraging her to drive in the opposite direction altogether. To put as many miles between herself and Polcarrow as it was possible to achieve in one day.

Because what was she going to say when Aunt Grace asked, as she surely would, if she'd met anyone in the village?

There was no point in fibbing, or pretence. News of her confrontation with Ross would soon filter back anyway, she thought, grimacing. Because that was how village life worked, which was why she couldn't wait to get back to the city, and its comparative anonymity.

If she had indeed encountered Ross in London it would have been no one's business but her own, and she could have handled it better there. Couldn't she? Or was she just fooling herself? Wouldn't it have provoked exactly the same wretched, inescapable memories?

And just how long would it be before she would finally be able to forget—to put behind her for ever their short-lived passionate marriage and the nightmare of disillusion which had followed it?

After all, she had just proved to herself beyond all doubt that every detail of their relationship was still only too fresh in her mind, she thought, biting her lip savagely.

Well, she would get through the wedding as best she could, and wearing a smile, too, even if she had to nail it there. And then she would go away somewhere and begin the entire healing process all over again.

Somehow she would find the means to come to terms with the situation once and for all, and this time she would succeed. Because there was no other choice open to her. Except despair, and that she would not allow. She'd been down that road before, and she would not—could not tread there again.

Especially when Ross had made it clear that he'd put their relationship behind him and that his new life was already in place.

She tried to cheer herself with the reflection that any lunchtime inquisition was bound to be inhibited by the presence of Adrian, and, of course, the unknown Tim. Her potential saviour. Or at least another focus for her attention for a few necessary hours.

Someone to chat and laugh and dance with at the wedding. Someone with whom she could pretend to be carefree, and even available.

And, hopefully, the demands of hospitality would also divert her aunt's attention from the vexed question of her shorn hair, she thought, touching the silky strands with a protective hand.

Also, with the arrival of the groom and best man, the wedding would take over to the exclusion of everything else. The countdown would begin, giving her, she prayed, no time to brood.

The last few days before her own marriage had merged into a kind of blur through which she'd floated in a blissful dream, thinking of nothing but the moment when she would belong to Ross at last and for ever.

She had never felt so cherished or desired in her life. No bridal nerves or last-minute doubts had troubled her either, in spite of the openly expressed anxieties of family and friends, who had begged both of them to extend the length of their engagement.

'But why should we wait?' she'd appealed to Uncle Henry. 'I thought you at least would understand. I thought you liked Ross.'

'I do, my dear.' He was silent for a moment. Frowning a little. 'But I'm not sure you have the same objectives in this marriage. At least not yet. Your aim is making a home, having a family with the man you love.'

'Is that so wrong?' she asked, hurt.

'No,' he said. 'But Ross, I think, only wants you. And that's not the same thing at all.'

To Jenna's additional distress, Natasha was not even going to be there, but was spending the weekend in Vienna. She had apologised, claiming it had been booked for ages, but Jenna wasn't convinced. The older girl had never openly expressed her disapproval, apart from that first morning, but it was always there, like a shadow, just the same.

Each time Jenna spent the night with Ross, she was aware, the following day, of Natasha's narrowed gaze assessing her almost tangible glow of fulfilment. And this had created an awkwardness that, for the first time in their relationship, simmered on the edge of resentment.

But that might be because her flatmate's own love life didn't seem to be going too swimmingly, Jenna reminded herself. She had overheard her talking on the phone one day at the gallery, her voice low and intense.

'How dare you treat me like this? I won't just be brushed aside from your life,' she'd been saying.

Jenna, embarrassed, had made herself scarce. As she'd brewed some coffee in the tiny kitchen, she had found herself wondering if Tasha had become involved with yet another married man.

Hasn't she learned by now that there's no future in such relationships? She'd thought, with an inward sigh. Just heartache?

She had never been able to understand why Natasha had no one permanent in her life. She was beautiful and intelligent, but though she always had plenty of dates none of them seemed to develop into a steady relationship.

Jenna, puzzled, had asked her once what she was looking for in a man, and the older girl had shrugged.

'When I find it,' she'd countered. 'I'll let you know.'

Leaving Jenna none the wiser.

She'd been genuinely anxious at the beginning for Ross and Natasha to meet, and had counted on them liking each other—for her sake, if no other. She'd told herself this would be bound to ease the situation.

But it had never happened. Their first encounter had been conducted in an atmosphere of hostility that had been almost tangible. Like two dogs circling each other, preparing for a fight, Jenna had recognised with astonishment. And things had never improved between them. At best, they treated each other with wary civility. At worst, it was like walking headlong into a wall of ice.

She'd had a desperate try at lightening things up by giving a dinner party, and Ross had brought along Seb Lithgow, a journalist friend, to make up the foursome. But it had still turned into another evening of forced conversation and awkward silences, even though Seb, who was tall, with dark blond hair and charm enough for several, had done his best.

An embarrassed Jenna had been aware that Natasha had barely exchanged two sentences with him.

'No more evenings like that, please,' Ross had said when they were alone.

'I know—it was awful.' She'd hugged him close, her face rueful. 'But she's in a funny mood these days. The hunt for my replacement isn't going too well, apparently.'

She'd expected some barbed rejoinder, but he'd said nothing. However, when she had glanced up at him she'd seen that his eyes were hooded and his mouth tight-lipped to the point of grimness.

In hindsight, Jenna could understand why the friction between them had existed.

Natasha must have seen right through him from day one, she told herself. And she knew, somehow, that he would break my heart. So she was just acting out of concern.

But when it happened, she never once said *I told you so*, and I'm so grateful to her for that.

She turned into the drive and parked on the gravelled sweep in front of the house, beside Adrian's Porsche.

There was a buzz of conversation coming from the drawing room, so she took a deep breath, nerving herself to push open the door and walk in as if nothing had happened.

Adrian was the first to spot her, and he strode over, grinning broadly, lifting her off her feet and kissing her soundly.

'What a transformation,' he commented as he put her down. 'Very chic, sweetheart. What's brought this on?'

Jenna touched her hair with a self-conscious hand. 'I felt a change was long overdue, that's all.'

'Well, it's absolutely terrific,' Christy said as she joined them, handing Jenna a glass of sherry. 'And it makes you look even younger, if that's possible.'

Jenna turned to Mrs Penloe. 'You see, Aunt Grace. Short hair suits me.'

'If you say so, dear,' said her aunt. 'I'm sure you had your reasons for having it cut—and of course it will always grow back again.'

Jenna exchanged a resigned look with Christy, then glanced round the drawing room.

'So, Adrian, where's this best friend of yours that I've yet to meet?'

'You'll have to wait until tomorrow for that,' Adrian said cheerfully. 'He wasn't feeling particularly great yesterday, so he decided to give it another twenty-four hours.'

'It must have been a hell of a stag night,' Jenna teased.

Adrian shook his head wryly. 'Not at all. A crowd of us went out for quite a sedate dinner, and I really didn't think Tim had drunk that much. Unless he started again once we got home,' he added with a frown. 'But he's sworn that he'll catch the early train and be here in time for the rehearsal tomorrow afternoon, hungover or not.' He grinned at Jenna. 'I've given you the big build-up, honey, so he's dying to meet you.'

Jenna forced a cheerful smile in response. 'Sounds promising.'

Just as she'd hoped, the wedding was the sole topic of conversation over lunch, and when the meal was over Adrian had a stack of wedding presents to bring in from the car, to be opened and admired, and put with all the others in the morning room.

'You've had some lovely things,' said Mrs Penloe. 'And so many of them, too,' she added worriedly. 'The two of you should sit down quietly this afternoon and make a list of them, with their donors, in case any of the cards get mislaid later on in the excitement.'

Jenna took one look at Adrian's face and bit back a smile. 'Why don't I do that?' she suggested. 'While you take Christy for a drive. Enjoy the calm before the storm.'

He grinned at her. 'You're an angel.'

Watching Aunt Grace bustling around with a sheaf of papers in her hand, her glasses on top of her head, muttering worriedly, Jenna realised with affection that she was in her element.

Of course, she'd seen her in action before, she reminded herself as she went into the morning room and started the list.

Once her aunt had seen that Ross and Jenna were not going to be deterred from their hasty marriage she'd moved into another gear.

Jenna had been perfectly ready to have a simple London ceremony in front of a registrar, but Aunt Grace had put her foot down with a firmness that brooked no further argument.

Jenna, she had said, would be married from the parish church in her own home village.

From then on her niece had watched in awe as Mrs Penloe had bullied the local bakery into making a cake, contacted a florist, discovered a catering company who had an unexpected gap on their calendar, and briskly despatched Jenna and Christy to an upmarket dress-hire boutique.

There had been no time for a full-blown reception, with a dance in the evening. As the wedding was to be sandwiched between photographic assignments to which he had already committed, Ross was taking his bride to Brittany for their brief honeymoon, and they'd need to catch an afternoon ferry.

They had stood together, the day before, watching the small round marquee, with its blue and white stripes, being erected briskly on the lawn.

'Heaven knows where Aunt Grace found it, but isn't it sweet?' Jenna leaned back into Ross's embrace. 'It looks like one of those little tents they used to have at medieval jousts.'

There was a smile in his voice. 'You're not expecting me to arrive at the church on horseback, carrying a lance, I hope?'

'Not unless you want to upset all Aunt Grace's arrangements and see her turn into a dragon.' She paused. 'If we'd lived in those days, would you have fought for me?'

His lips touched her hair. 'Against all the world.'

And I believed him, Jenna thought flatly. I thought we'd belong together for ever. I had all the confidence in the world.

Thirza had called to see her that evening, she remembered, wearing a striking silk dress in one of her own exotic prints and bringing with her a flat leather case.

'I don't know whether you subscribe to the old superstitions,' she said, 'but I've brought you something old.'

Jenna gasped when she opened the case and saw the string of gleaming pearls lying on a black velvet bed.

'But they're beautiful. How can you bear to part with them?'

Thirza shrugged. 'They're not my style. Besides, they belonged to Ross's mother originally, and I decided long ago to keep them for his wife.'

Jenna touched them almost reverently. 'I truly don't know what to say. How to thank you.'

Thirza shrugged. 'Just make him happy,' she said abruptly. 'If you can.'

Jenna gasped. 'Of course I shall.'

'I'm sure you think so,' the older woman returned more gently. 'But there are a lot of adjustments to be made on both sides, and it's not going to be easy.' She paused. 'He tells me he's decided to give up overseas assignments and run the London desk at the agency. That's quite a sacrifice.'

Jenna lifted her chin. 'It was his own idea. I didn't ask him to do it.'

'No, but you didn't tell him not to, either,' Thirza said crisply. She shook her head. 'Jenna, I know your father went away and didn't come back, and for that I'm truly sorry. But you can't compensate by keeping Ross tied at home. It doesn't work like that. And he's not a substitute either.'

Jenna bit her lip. She said stiffly, 'That— never even occurred to me.'

'I'm glad to hear it. But please think about what I've said,' Thirza urged. 'It's not too late for him to change his mind.'

'It's Ross's own decision,' Jenna defended.

Thirza sighed. 'As you wish. But you'd do better to let Ross have his freedom now, while he's still flying high. I promise you it won't be a problem in the long term. He'll be even keener to settle down if you don't clip his wings now.'

'Why don't you say all this to him?'

'I already did.' Thirza gave a tight-lipped smile. 'And now, having put your back up permanently for the best possible motives, I'd better go before you throw me out. Enjoy your day tomorrow. I'm sure you'll make an exquisite bride.'

And she went, leaving Jenna staring after her.

Perhaps she was right, Jenna thought now, trying to decipher the name scrawled on a card accompanying a Lalique figure. Maybe I did try and tie him down to domesticity too soon. But if I'd turned him loose, in all probability he would simply have been unfaithful that much sooner.

Presumably, Thirza herself had been prepared to put up with that kind of treatment from his father.

Perhaps those were the adjustments she told me I'd need to make. Only I wouldn't. I couldn't.

Not when I was already at my lowest ebb anyway, after losing the baby.

The child Ross didn't even want.

I should have remembered pearls are for tears and left them in their case.

Her throat tightened uncontrollably and she hunted in her pocket for a tissue and blew her nose.

I was crazy to come here, she thought wretchedly. Mad to put myself through this all over again.

And I'm going to be counting the hours until I can turn my back on this place and its memories, and rejoin the real world.

They weren't dining at home that night. They were joining Adrian at the Fisherman's Arms in Polcarrow, where he and Tim would be staying until the wedding.

Jenna had a relaxing soak in the tub, then applied her favourite scented body lotion. She kept her make-up light, then put on one of her favourite dresses—a plain slip style in a silky apple green fabric, with narrow straps and a skirt cleverly cut on the bias. Her sandals were green, too, and she flung a silvery pashmina round her shoulders.

'Very elfin,' Christy said approvingly when she saw her. 'What a pity Tim isn't around to be led astray.'

'Oh, I'm fresh out of fairy dust,' Jenna said lightly. 'Did you have a pleasant afternoon?'

Christy blushed revealingly, indicating that the drive out had probably only taken them as far as Adrian's room at the hotel. 'You could say that.' She paused. 'I hope Ma didn't get too heavy about everything.'

'She found a number of little jobs for me,' Jenna admitted. 'But at least they stopped me from being bored.' *Or thinking…*

The hotel was a popular venue for diners, specialising as it did in fresh fish and seafood, and most of the tables in the low-ceilinged room were already occupied when the party from Trevarne House arrived, to be given prime position in the big bow window which overlooked the harbour.

And Adrian had arranged for champagne on ice to be waiting for them at their table.

'How splendid,' Mrs Penloe said happily as she sat down. 'You're spoiling us, my dear.'

'It's a time for celebration,' Adrian returned as the wine waiter removed the cork and filled their glasses. 'We're all together—and for the best of reasons. So let's drink to that.'

'Not quite all of us,' Christy objected. 'Tim's not here, remember.'

'All right,' her fiancé said, unperturbed. 'We'll drink to ''absent friends'' instead.' And he raised his glass.

The words sent an odd shiver crawling down Jenna's spine. A goose, she thought, walking over her grave...

'Oh, no, not that.' Her voice was raised and slightly brittle. She flushed as they all looked at her in surprise. 'I mean—we can do that later. But first I'd much rather drink to you and Christy,' she went on, stumbling a little. 'To— to your happiness.'

'Then we shall,' her uncle said quietly. 'To Christy and Adrian. May love be long and life be kind.'

As he spoke he glanced at his wife and smiled, and she put her hand gently on his sleeve.

He was describing his own marriage, Jenna thought, a lump in her throat as she watched them. An affection that had remained un-dimmed down the years.

And yet, on the face of it, they weren't the most obvious of soulmates. He quiet, humor-ous and laid back, happy to be semi-retired from his successful architectural practice and pursuing his passion for Cornish history. Aunt Grace more volatile and sociable, always busy, too, revelling in her involvement in local af-fairs and organisations.

But it worked, Jenna acknowledged with a small inward sigh. Oh, God, how it worked. And made the failure of her own marriage more poignant by comparison.

But she was not here to be the skeleton at the feast, she reminded herself forcefully, but to enjoy the food and company. And she would do exactly that, or die in the attempt.

And champagne was always a good start, she told herself, relishing its dry chill against the tightness of her throat as she accepted the menu she was being handed with murmured thanks.

She'd decided on griddled scallops and king prawns with rice for her main course, and was hesitating between gazpacho and red pepper mousse as a starter when she was aware of a stir in the restaurant and glanced up casually.

She stiffened, her hands tightening their grip on the leather-bound menu until the knuckles turned white, as she watched with utter disbelief Thirza threading her way through the restaurant, with Ross one pace behind her.

One swift glance around her revealed her aunt and uncle exchanging appalled glances and Christy sitting frozen, her bottom lip caught in her teeth, while Adrian muttered something under his breath.

There was only one unoccupied table, she realised swiftly, and that, thankfully, was in the opposite corner of the room—about as far away as it was possible to get.

She paused, her heart thudding in sudden panic, as Thirza suddenly changed track and came towards the window table and its transfixed occupants. She looked magnificent, in an ankle-length indigo dress topped by a loose floating jacket, blocked in jewel colours like a stained glass window, as she loomed over them all. Ross waited a few feet away, his face saturnine, his hooded eyes unreadable.

'Henry—Grace—what a marvellous surprise.' Her voice carried through the room. 'A cosy little family party. How are you, Christy? Adrian, you're looking well.' A pause. 'Good evening Jenna.'

There was an awkward chorus of responses.

'Thirza, my dear.' Henry Penloe had risen politely. 'How good to see you. I didn't know this was one of your haunts.'

'It isn't, but I felt poor Ross needed a break from my cooking.' She was laughing, gesturing expansively. 'After all, he's supposed to be convalescing, and I don't want to make him ill again.'

Another pause, and Jenna felt suddenly as if she was on the edge of a precipice.

Then, 'I see,' Thirza said, smiling, 'that the table is laid for six. Are you expecting another guest?'

'We were,' Mr Penloe returned. 'A friend of Adrian's. But unfortunately he's been delayed until tomorrow.'

'Then why don't we get Carlo to lay an additional place and join you? After all, we're family, too, don't forget.'

There couldn't be a soul in the room unaware that some kind of drama was being played out, Jenna thought bitterly. And Thirza had stage-managed it beautifully, making it impossible for the Penloes to refuse. But why? *Why?*

Christy rose to the occasion. 'Of course,' she said brightly. 'If we all move round a little there'll be plenty of room.' And in that way Jenna would be safely flanked by her uncle on one side and Adrian on the other, was her unspoken message.

Chairs were shifted, the head waiter summoned, cutlery and glassware brought, and the thing was accomplished. And Jenna found herself vulnerable in a different way, facing Ross across the table.

But apart from a cool smile, and a murmured acknowledgement of her presence when he first sat down, he paid her no direct attention at all, chatting instead, with apparent ease, to Christy and Mrs Penloe.

And then there were food orders to be taken, and wines to be chosen, which did away with any potential awkward silences. Although Thirza would not have allowed those anyway. From the first she set out to be the life and soul of the party, chatting and laughing about her curtailed trip to Australia.

Under cover of a sprightly description of Alice Springs, Adrian said quietly, 'I'm sorry about this, Jenna.'

'It's not your fault. My uncle calls Thirza a law unto herself. A force of nature.'

'I'm sure he's right. However, I wasn't referring to her but to your ex-husband.'

'Well, don't worry about him.' Jenna smiled tautly. 'Didn't Christy tell you that an armistice has been declared for the duration of the wedding?'

'She mentioned something, yes, but it sounded iffy to me.'

'Oh, it's perfectly genuine, I assure you.' She managed a shrug. 'Besides, Ross being around really doesn't bother me any more. I'm through with all that now.'

'Really?' Adrian's smile was kind but sceptical. 'Anything you say, sweetheart.'

She was glad to turn to Uncle Henry, who engaged her in a gentle flow of chat about a book he was considering writing on some of the Duchy's great houses and their architecture. That, and the arrival of the food, should have been enough to distract her, but in reality nothing seemed able to dispel her tingling, uneasy awareness of the man sitting on the opposite side of the table.

Across the central cluster of candles and flowers she could feel him watching her. Could sense unerringly that his eyes were studying her face—then moving down to the first swell of her breasts above the low neckline of her dress, just as they'd done so many times before. And now, as then, she felt her skin warming helplessly under his scrutiny.

What the hell did he think he was doing? she raged inwardly. Or was it just an automatic reflex when he was confronted by a woman—any woman?

Whatever the reason, he was not, she thought bitterly, playing fair. But, then, what was new about that?

Her best—her only response was to appear oblivious to his regard, but this was easier to decide than perform, because that familiar trembling ache was stirring into life again deep inside her. A response that, to her shame, he had always been able to evoke, even when their relationship had been falling apart.

The food was delicious, but Jenna had to force herself to eat and echo the appreciative noises from her neighbours. Ross, a lightning glance told her, had no such problem, but appeared to be enjoying every mouthful of his sea bass.

When the dessert menus appeared she was able to say with perfect truth that she couldn't manage another thing. On the other hand Ross, she noted crossly, asked for the cheeseboard.

'It's so good to see him eating at last,' Thirza proclaimed. 'He needs to build his strength up after that awful illness,' she added, looking round fiercely as if daring them to contradict her.

'How long do you plan to stay in Cornwall, Ross?' Mr Penloe asked quietly.

'I'm seeing the consultant next week,' Ross returned. 'Once he gives me the all-clear I can start finalising my plans.'

'You must be keen to get back to work,' Christy commented.

His smile was cool. 'Of course, but that's only part of it.' He paused. 'I'm hoping to be married again quite soon.'

There was a shocked, deafening silence. Under cover of the tablecloth Jenna's hands were clenched together so tightly that she could have cried out from the pain. So, she thought, that was that. And she couldn't say she hadn't been warned.

She realised that everyone was studiously not looking at her—apart from Ross, who was leaning back in his chair, an unsmiling challenge in his dark eyes.

A challenge that she had to meet—and fast. She lifted her chin. 'Congratulations.' Her tone was light, almost amused. 'Your plans weren't quite so finite when you mentioned them this morning. That's—quite a step forward.'

'The world's an uncertain place,' he said. 'Life can be short and brutal. So—I talked things over with her, and a decision was made.'

'That's really good news.' The words scraped her throat like sharp knives. She lifted her glass. 'Here's to better luck—the second time around.'

She paused. 'For both of us.'

'Why, Jen...' Christy's face was bewildered. 'Have you met someone, too? How marvellous. You never mentioned it.'

Jenna shrugged. 'Oh, it's early days. And, anyway, I'm enjoying the single life.' She met Ross's gaze. 'I have no plans to remarry. I think it's an unnecessary complication.'

She was lying—continually and desperately. Trying to shield herself from the devastating and unwelcome truth that had just exploded in her mind.

The realisation that, in spite of everything that had happened between them—all the harrowing sadness and betrayal in their relationship—she was indeed a one-man woman, and always would be.

And, heaven help her, Ross was the one and only man she would ever want.

A man, she acknowledged, that she had just lost for ever.

And somehow, however agonising it might be, she was going to have to find some way to go on living without him.

CHAPTER FIVE

JENNA never knew how she got through the rest of the meal. From some depth of her being she managed to dredge up the ability to stay outwardly composed, and even radiate charm and interest in what was going on around her.

She chatted and laughed, and even accepted admiring tastes of other people's desserts, when all she really wanted to do was crawl into some dark and deserted space and howl her shock and wretchedness to the moon.

How could she possibly still care for someone who had behaved so badly and so callously? she asked herself with wincing incredulity. How could anyone be such a pathetic fool?

She told herself with increasing desperation that it must be a delusion. Had to be. That seeing Ross again so unexpectedly—being thrown together with him like this—had knocked her sideways. Made her a little crazy.

That could be the only feasible explanation for the chaos of her thoughts.

And, yes, she still wanted him physically. That was something she could no longer deny.

His lovemaking had created this burning hunger in her, and for many long months it had gone unsatisfied, leaving her sexually bereft. Now, as she had discovered to her cost, simply being near him was enough to light the fire all over again. And her suffering was exquisite. Unbearable.

She'd looked at him this evening, sitting across the table from her in all the formality of a dark suit and silk tie, and had a vision of him leaning over her naked, his eyes drowsy with passion, his mouth warm as it sought hers in the long, sweet prelude to possession.

In those first months of loving, his body had become as familiar to her as her own, and her hands had memorised him with rapturous joy, lingering over the strength of bone and play of muscle, making him groan softly with desire in turn.

And now some other unknown girl would arch in pleasure beneath him and cry out wordlessly at the culmination, and the knowledge of that was tearing her apart. Someone else would have his baby and he would probably never remember, in his new-found delight, that there had once been the prospect of another child. Short-lived. With her.

And, for her, an ever-present pain.

Her nails scored the palms of her hand beneath the shelter of the cloth. She thought, I need to get out of here. I want to be on my own. But there was little chance of that. When they arrived back at Trevarne House both Christy and Aunt Grace would be eager to discuss the evening, and Ross's startling revelation.

And somehow she would have to pretend that it didn't matter. That, for her, it was a positive step, drawing a final and much needed line under her brief marriage. But how long would she be able to sustain this charade of indifference when, emotionally, she was coming apart at the seams?

Also, she supposed dully, she would have to admit to the Penloes that there was no one in her own life, after all. That what she'd implied was simply a face-saving exercise. They would understand, of course, because they loved her, and were loyal. But then they would expect her to move on, too. To follow Ross's example and establish a new relationship. To seize a second chance at happiness.

And only she knew how impossible that was.

She was thankful to see her uncle signalling for the bill, but less happy when Ross intercepted it on its arrival at the table, tossing his credit card on to the salver.

'No, I insist.' His smile was faintly tight-lipped as Mr Penloe and Adrian protested. 'After all, we were the intruders on a private family occasion. This is by way of amends.'

Emphasising that, no matter what Thirza might say, he no longer considered himself part of the family since the divorce, Jenna thought with a pang.

She trailed in the rear as they left the restaurant, and waited unobtrusively while good-nights were being said—Aunt Grace constrained and faintly on her dignity, she noted with reluctant amusement. But any hopes of a speedy exit were unfulfilled when Adrian was called away to the telephone by the receptionist.

And, to her dismay, she saw Ross coming towards her.

'I wanted to thank you,' he said abruptly. 'Your comments just now were—generous.'

He paused. 'Maybe the truce could last beyond the wedding. What do you think?'

'I don't really see the necessity.' Jenna met his gaze coolly. 'I think a clean break divorce should be exactly that. And nothing's changed.'

'"Shake hands for ever. Cancel all our vows,"' Ross quoted softly. 'Is that how you see it?'

'No,' she said. 'That's how it really is. Subtle difference.'

'Some divorced couples manage to remain friendly,' he said meditatively. 'And no one can have too many friends, Jenna.'

She shook her head, looking past him, noting almost absently that Adrian had emerged from the phone booth looking strangely agitated.

'We were never friends, Ross,' she said. 'Perhaps that was part of the trouble.'

'Ah,' he said softly. 'The trouble. What a multitude of sins that could be said to cover.'

He paused. 'You know, Jenna, I'd really like to get together with you one day soon and have a look at everything that happened between us. The retrospective viewpoint can sometimes be valuable—don't you think?'

'No,' she said tautly, 'I don't. History was never one of my favourite subjects.'

He smiled faintly. 'And that's what we are?'

'Of course,' she said. 'And it's time to move on. Look forward, not back, and get on with our lives.' Keep saying it—repeating it, she thought, and maybe one day it will come to mean something.

'Difficult,' he said. 'When there's so much unfinished business to resolve.'

'Consider it done,' she said. 'I had a miscarriage. You had an affair.' She managed a shrug. 'End of story.'

He said slowly, 'I said just now you were generous, but apparently that's a quality you reserve for public occasions.'

'And there aren't many more of those to go.' She lifted her chin. 'Once Christy and Adrian are married we won't be meeting again.'

'That's if there is a wedding,' Ross remarked, his brows drawing together. 'There seems to be some kind of fuss going on over there, and your cousin is in tears.'

'Oh, God, so she is.' Trying not to be thankful that she was off the hook, Jenna flew to Christy's side. 'Darling—what is it?'

'It's Tim,' Adrian replied tersely, his arm protectively round his weeping fiancée. 'That was his mother on the phone. It seems he wasn't hungover at all. It was chicken pox, and he can't make the wedding.' He attempted a rueful grin. 'So, as of this moment, I don't have a best man.'

'Oh, my dear,' said Mrs Penloe. 'Surely one of your other friends…?'

Adrian shrugged unhappily. 'Maybe, but it's a hell of a thing to dump on someone at the last minute. There's the speech, for one thing. I can ring around in the morning, but quite a few of them will be already on their way down.' He shook his head. 'Thank God I brought the rings with me.' He delved into a pocket and produced a handkerchief, and began to dry Christy's eyes. 'Don't cry any more, darling. We'll sort something out, I promise.'

'Ross can do it,' said Thirza.

There was an astonished silence.

Jenna felt a sudden roaring in her ears. The word *No* was pounding so violently at her consciousness that she thought she might have shouted it aloud.

But Aunt Grace was the first to speak. 'I hardly think so, Thirza dear,' she said with unwonted frostiness. 'As you pointed out at dinner, Ross is still recovering from a serious illness, and would hardly wish to take on so much responsibility so soon.'

Ross looked across at Jenna, his mouth twisting sardonically—as if in acknowledgement of the inner disquiet that only he could see.

'Damn you,' she whispered under her breath. 'Damn you to hell.'

He said coolly, 'I hardly think it will bring on a relapse, Mrs Penloe, but thanks for your concern.' He paused. 'As it happens, I'd be happy to do it, if Adrian agrees.'

'Well, of course he agrees,' Thirza said impatiently. 'It's the obvious—the only solution.'

'A morning suit.' Aunt Grace was battling bravely on. 'What are we going to do about that? Unless by some amazing coincidence he happens to have one with him,' she added with a touch of edge.

'I don't possess that amount of foresight,' Ross said drily. 'But I can hire one. It's not a problem.'

'As a matter of fact,' Adrian said slowly, 'I brought Tim's suit down with me, and I think you're pretty much the same size.' He paused. 'You could always try it and see.'

A flushed Christy parted her lips to speak, caught Jenna's eye, and subsided.

'That's fine with me.' Ross's gaze swept the stunned semi-circle in front of him. 'Unless anyone has any further objections.'

Jenna cut in smoothly, before Aunt Grace could launch herself again. She was trapped, and she knew it, and so did he. All that remained was damage limitation. The maintenance of the pretence she'd been forced into.

'On the contrary, it seems the ideal arrangement,' she said. She even made herself smile. 'It's really good of you, Ross, to fill the breach like this.'

He said softly, 'It will be my pleasure, believe me.' He turned to Adrian. 'Should we have a look at that suit now? Just in case I need to make an early start with the hire companies?'

'Er—yes. Absolutely.' Adrian gave Christy a swift kiss and an anxious look. 'I'll see you in the morning, darling.' And he and Ross disappeared towards the stairs.

Uncle Henry muttered something about fetching the car, and Mrs Penloe and Christy followed him to the door.

Leaving Jenna momentarily alone with Thirza. Their glances met—clashed—leaving Jenna in no doubt that here was someone else she hadn't fooled by her acquiescence.

She drew a deep breath. 'What exactly do you think you've been doing tonight?' she demanded shakily.

'Righting a few wrongs.' Thirza's tone was steely. 'I've had enough of seeing my stepson treated as a pariah while the world tiptoes round you, the poor little victim.'

Jenna sank her teeth into her lower lip. 'I wasn't the one who ended the marriage,' she said. 'I didn't have the affair.'

'I don't condone what Ross did.' Thirza's mouth tightened. 'But the marriage was in trouble long before he went astray. Think about that, princess, next time you feel like shining up your sense of grievance.'

Jenna said thickly, 'You've always taken his side.'

The older woman shrugged. 'Someone had to,' she retorted brusquely. 'Why wasn't it you, Jenna?'

And she turned away and walked into the bar, leaving Jenna, white-faced and speechless, staring after her.

Jenna sat on the window seat in her bedroom, leaning her aching forehead against the chill of the glass and staring unseeingly into the darkness. She wanted to sleep. She needed to sleep. But she knew it wasn't going to happen. Not while her mind was teeming relentlessly like this.

How dared Thirza? she thought numbly. How dared she say those things? Imply that I was the one at fault?

The older woman's words had touched all kinds of nerves, and left her feeling sore and on edge. But it had been the earlier encounter with Ross which had done the most damage, she realised wretchedly.

She had been silent during the car ride home, but Aunt Grace had more than made up for it, inveighing bitterly against what she called 'that shameless intrusion'.

'And now Ross is going to be best man,' she'd added bitterly. 'What can Adrian be thinking of?'

'Of the difficulty of finding someone else at such short notice,' said Christy bleakly. 'Even I can see that. And if Jenna says she doesn't mind, why should we?' She shook her head. 'Oh, I could strangle Tim. How on earth does a grown man get chicken pox?'

The million-pound question, Jenna thought, biting her lip. The shield she'd hoped for was gone. Now all she had to rely on was her own resources.

And the fact that they were now playing opposite each other in leading roles at the wedding was bound to attract the sort of attention she'd desperately hoped to avoid.

'Oh, God,' she groaned under her breath. 'What am I going to do?'

Back at the house, she silently shared coffee and recriminations with the others for a while, then concocted a series of elaborate yawns, announced she was dead on her feet, and went thankfully upstairs.

On the landing, she encountered Uncle Henry. She was about to slip past with a murmured 'Goodnight' when he detained her with a gentle hand on her arm.

'Jenna, my dear.' His voice was kind. 'I can probably put a stop to this situation, if that's what you wish.'

'But I don't,' she said, too quickly. She gave him a resolute smile. 'It's going to prove to everyone, once and for all, that Ross and I have agreed to put our—difficulties behind us.'

'And become just good friends?' Her uncle's expression was quizzical.

Jenna hesitated. 'Well, not that, perhaps. But maybe we can turn our differences into indifference. That would be a positive step.'

'And is that what Ross wants, too?'

Jenna bit her lip. 'I have no idea—what Ross wants.'

Mr Penloe gave a quick sigh. 'No,' he said. 'Probably not. But it's something you might choose to consider—even now, at this late stage.' He patted her on the shoulder and went on his way.

Jenna was frowning as she went into her room and closed the door behind her. Was Uncle Henry also hinting that she hadn't been completely an innocent party in the breakdown of her marriage? Surely not, she thought in bewilderment. She'd always known she could count on his sympathy and support ever since she'd first come to live at Trevarne House. All these years, he'd been her rock.

Now, once again, she felt as if the ground was shivering under her feet.

She undressed, putting on her nightgown and her robe, but she made no attempt to get into bed, although she switched off the light to give the deliberate impression that she was already asleep and deter late-night visitors. Much as she loved Christy and Aunt Grace, she acknowledged ruefully, she didn't want to talk any more about what had happened, or how it would affect the wedding.

It was still too raw in her mind. Besides, she could only think about what it was likely to do to herself. She couldn't summon up enough generosity of spirit to take the broader view.

In fact, she couldn't find much spirit at all, she thought wearily. Over the past couple of days she seemed to have taken one blow after another.

And the worst of them all was tonight's recognition of her own terrible weakness.

Since the breakdown of their marriage, out of the morass of heartbreak and bitterness, had come the conviction that she hated Ross, and always would. Over the months it had become her armour and salvation. Yet, when put to the test, it had proved no protection at all.

Now I only hate myself for still wanting him, she thought, wrapping her arms convulsively round her shivering body. And I despise myself, too. Especially as I know beyond doubt that this need is totally one-sided.

But then it probably always had been...

She'd told herself from the very first that to forgive Ross was out of the question and to forget was equally impossible. Yet the sobering fact was she'd been called on for neither option.

When she'd confronted him, accusing him of having slept with Lisa Weston, she'd expected him to deny it. Had prayed that he'd offer proof of his innocence.

Instead he'd acknowledged his transgression, coolly and frankly, expressing regret but offering no excuse or even explanation for his conduct. Leaving her stricken to the heart.

Presumably, Jenna thought wearily, he'd been convinced that he wouldn't be found out, and that he could continue to live his bachelor life within the framework of marriage.

And when, shocked and humiliated, she'd ordered him, weeping, out of the house and her life, he'd turned and left without a single word of protest.

She'd told herself that he would return in a few days, asking for another chance, and that no matter how much he begged and pleaded she would not take him back. That justice demanded he should be made to suffer as she was doing.

Only he'd never come back, and the certainty that it was not an isolated fall from grace—that he was now permanently with his mistress—had pushed the knife deeper and twisted it. Forcing her to face the reality that she'd been fooling herself. That her marriage was over, almost as soon as it had begun. That all those dire warnings had been perfectly justified.

I truly thought we were happy, she told herself desolately. At least until we lost the baby.

Not that we agreed on everything, of course, but, then, who does? I thought it was all part of learning to live together. So when did it all start to unravel in earnest?

If she was honest, she had to admit that Ross had been something of an enigma from the first. There were whole layers of his life that he had chosen not to disclose, or not immediately, anyway.

He had been still very young when his mother died, but from comments he had made she'd gathered that his parents' relationship had been a stormy one, and he'd been fully aware of this.

And when, barely two years later, he'd found himself with Thirza as his stepmother, it had proved no different.

Jenna had learned that Ross's father had been a serial womaniser, who'd also liked to gamble, and that as a result, Ross's maternal grandparents had quarrelled with their daughter Marina at the time of her marriage and continued to stay aloof after her death.

It was through them, however, that he'd acquired Les Roches, the old stone house on the Brittany coast where Jenna had spent her brief, idyllic honeymoon.

'My great-grandfather was a fisherman,' he'd told her. 'And Grand-mère Marianne was his only child. She met my grandfather during the war, when he was with the SOE and she was helping the Resistance.'

Jenna's eyes widened. 'How very romantic.'

'I doubt that,' Ross said wryly. 'Dirty, dangerous and bloody terrifying, I'd have said. But when the war was over he came back for her. And when she inherited the house they used it as a holiday retreat.'

'And then they left it to you—their only grandson?'

Ross shrugged. 'Under French law they had little choice,' he returned drily.

'But you were reconciled with them after your father died?'

'To a limited extent, but we were never really close. Too much had happened in the past. And they didn't really want anyone else. They were lovers all their lives, totally sufficient for each other.'

'Oh,' she said. Then, 'That's really—rather wonderful, isn't it?'

'Is it?' His mouth twisted.

'Yes,' she said. 'Of course. And that's exactly how we'll be, too.'

'You really think lightning can strike twice—in the same family?'

'I'm sure it can.' She spoke defiantly.

'If you say so.' He kissed her troubled mouth. 'Poor Jenna. You want the world to be neat and tidy, with no dark corners or skeletons in cupboards. And it isn't like that. It can't be.'

She sighed. 'You're laughing at me.' She paused. 'Are you talking about yourself? Do you have a skeleton in your cupboard, Ross?'

'Dozens of them.' He pulled her closer, his mouth teasing on hers, then suddenly hungry. 'So beware what doors you open, my love.'

And I, Jenna thought, wincing, was fool enough to believe he was joking.

Their marriage service had been simple but beautiful, using the words of the old prayer book. As she made her vows Jenna had felt a rush of emotion that seemed to lift her to a higher sphere.

She was going to make him happy, she had resolved passionately. Happier than he had ever dreamed. And people would look at their marriage and sigh with envy.

It had been dark when they'd arrived at Les Roches, and Jenna had been too tired after the excitement of the day, and a Channel crossing that had been less than tranquil, to pay much attention to her surroundings.

She'd been dimly aware of flagged stone floors, pale walls and low ceilings as Ross had guided her up the steep staircase. The bedroom was raftered, with fur rugs on the wooden floor and the window open to the sound of the sea. The bed was enormous, with carved head and foot boards, and the crisp linen was scented with lavender.

'It's very old,' Ross told her softly. 'A proper *lit matrimoniale*. My ancestors, as you see, took their marital duties very seriously.'

'And do you plan to follow their example?' she whispered back.

'Certainly,' he said. 'But not tonight.'

'Why not?' She did not hide her disappointment.

'Because it's been a long day,' he said simply. 'And I want to lie, holding you in my arms as you sleep. Enjoying being your husband at last. We have all the time in the world to make love, my beautiful wife, but tonight I want to cherish you, just as I promised a few hours ago.'

He undressed her slowly, his hands gentle. Slipped over her head the folds of the cobweb nightgown she'd never thought she'd wear and lifted her into the waiting bed. Swiftly he shed his own clothes and joined her, drawing her into his arms, against the lean warmth of his body.

Fighting her drowsiness, she said, 'But we have champagne...'

'We'll drink it later.' His lips caressed her hair, her closing eyelids. 'After all, my love, we have the rest of our lives. Now, sleep.'

And sleep she did. Deeply and dreamlessly, with her head pillowed on his chest.

When eventually she awoke, stretching languidly, the sun was pouring through the shutters and Ross was nowhere to be seen. She pushed back the duvet and slid out of bed. She padded to the door and called his name, but there was no answer.

Puzzled, she went to the window and opened the shutters, and it was then, as she turned back towards the bed, that she noticed the slip of paper pinned to the adjoining pillow and its laconic message— 'Gone shopping.'

Jenna showered swiftly in the large, old-fashioned bathroom, then pulled on a pair of white shorts and a pale pink cotton shirt which she tied under her midriff, slipping her feet into simple canvas shoes before descending the stairs.

The front door stood wide open, demonstrating that casual crime was not a consideration, and she went out into the sunshine and stood looking round her, lips parting in a gasp of delight.

Sheltered by a tall cliff, and standing on a broad jetty, with the sea glittering and dancing only a few yards away, Les Roches was a long, low house built in grey stone, which gave the impression that it had been hewn out of the living rock that guarded it. The shutters were a faded blue, and wooden tubs filled with summer blooms flanked the doorway.

Opposite, a flight of ancient stone steps, green with weed, led down to a crescent of beach.

Jenna drew a blissful breath, absorbing the salty tang in the air, listening to the cry of the gulls as they wheeled and swooped.

There were no other houses to be seen anywhere, and the steep access road, she realised, was little better than a track.

This, she thought, was seclusion of a very high order.

She heard the sound of an engine, and turned to see Ross's car descending towards her. She saw his smile through the windscreen and lifted her hand to wave in response, feeling suddenly and ridiculously shy.

He parked by the wall of the house and collected a series of bulging carriers from the boot, which he took into the house. It necessitated two trips.

When he finally emerged he came over to her, pulling her into his arms for a long, very thorough kiss.

'Good morning,' he murmured. 'Welcome to married life. I hope you appreciate how well-trained I am.'

'I'm seriously impressed.' She linked her arms round his neck. 'Are you stocking up for a siege?'

'Something like that.' His grin was slow and sexy. 'Let's say I don't see us travelling far from the house for a while.'

'And I thought you had a full sightseeing programme planned.' Jenna pretended to pout.

'Oh, I have.' He kissed her again. 'Starting almost at once.' He paused. 'Tell me, my sweet, are you wearing anything at all under this fetching outfit?'

'That,' she said, 'is a leading question.' She turned to look at the sea. 'This is a wonderful place.'

'I'm glad you approve. I wondered if you might find it too similar to Cornwall. If you'd have preferred a city break to another seascape.'

'Never.'

He slid his arms round her waist, his hands lifting to cup her breasts through the thin shirt, his thumbs teasing her nipples.

He said with a note of laughter in his voice, 'Did you sleep well.'

'Beautifully.' Jenna arched like a purring cat under his caress.

'And you're not tired any more?'

'Not even a little bit.' Her lips curved mischievously.

'I disagree.' He bit her earlobe very gently. 'I feel very strongly that you should go back to bed at once and stay there, while I provide tender loving care.'

'And will that make me feel better?' she asked demurely.

'I guarantee it.' His fingers slid inside the waistband of her shorts, stroking the warm flat plane of her stomach, then moving lower.

'And will I ever be cured?' Her voice was beginning to sound breathless.

'Never,' he said. 'Because I intend the treatment to last a lifetime.'

And he picked her up in his arms and carried her into the house, and up the stairs to where their marriage bed waited.

It was a day from Paradise. Jenna had thought that Ross had already shown her all that sexual pleasure could afford, but during the long, sweet hours that followed they seemed to ascend together to new, undreamed of heights. Any lingering inhibitions she might still have possessed vanished for ever as Ross's hands and lips coaxed her to a rapture so piercing she thought she might die.

And she gave as much back to him in turn, freely and glowingly, matching his overwhelming generosity.

And when, at last, she slept once more in his arms, spent and drained from passion, she was drowsily aware of his voice whispering that he loved her.

Much later, hunger drove them, laughing, down to the kitchen for bread, pâté and cheese, and the long-neglected champagne.

Later still, they took a bath together in the deep, elderly tub. Lying back in his arms,

Jenna said dreamily, 'I could stay here for ever.'

'I don't advise it.' Ross scooped up some scented foam and decorated the peaks of her breasts with judicious care. 'We'd get all white and wrinkly.'

She sighed. 'You're such a fool. I meant stay in this house. Live here.' She looked round at him. 'Why don't we?'

'Because we have careers—a life elsewhere.' He kissed the side of her neck, making the pulse quicken. 'This is an interlude, darling, and for now that's all it can be. After a while, the big world would beckon us back.'

She pulled a face. 'I suppose…'

'Hey.' Ross nibbled her damp shoulder. 'This is our honeymoon. You're supposed to be happy.'

'I'm delirious.' She snuggled closer to him. 'For one thing, I've just realised I'll never have to creep guiltily back to the flat ever again, running the gauntlet of Natasha's disapproval. I might even get to eat breakfast.'

There was a sudden tension in the arm that encircled her. 'Natasha gave you problems? You didn't tell me.'

'Well, nothing was ever said,' she admitted. 'At least, not out loud. But there was sometimes a bit of an atmosphere.' She sighed again. 'I wish she could find someone and be happy, too. Because she's so beautiful. Don't you think so?'

Ross turned her in his arms and kissed her mouth. He said quietly, 'I think you're beautiful, and that's all that matters.'

Eventually, they put on some clothes and went downstairs. Ross put the chicken he had bought in the stove to cook, while Jenna prepared the vegetables to accompany it.

While their evening meal was cooking they went for a stroll along the beach at the edge of the sea, where a glorious sunset promised more golden days to come.

As they walked back Jenna glanced over her shoulder and saw the imprint of their footsteps side by side in the damp sand.

It seemed like a good omen—a symbol of the journey they'd embarked on together, she decided, then laughed at herself inwardly for the sheer romanticism of the thought.

But when she reached the steps Jenna looked back and saw that the encroaching tide had covered the marks of their feet, erasing them as if they had never existed.

Transient, she thought. Not eternal.

And found, suddenly, she was shivering.

CHAPTER SIX

JENNA rose from the window seat and began to pace up and down the room.

They had indeed been golden days, she told herself. And she was thankful she hadn't known how few of them there were to be, or her heart would have broken right then and there.

Anyway, she should not be remembering how good things had once been between them. She should be reminding herself of how it had all collapsed in ruins. Rebuilding her defences.

But the temptation to relive that happy time in Brittany was overwhelming. The weather had been kind throughout their stay, and they'd swum in the sea and sunbathed on the beach, explored the surrounding countryside on foot and in the car. They both loved seafood, and Ross had introduced her to the joys of the great platters of *fruits de mer* that were a local speciality. Sometimes they'd cooked at home, but more often they'd visited one of the numerous small restaurants in the vicinity.

But most of the time they had been happy just being at Les Roches together in the private world they had created together.

In fact, learning to live with Ross had never been a problem, she reflected. There'd been differences in temperament, of course. He was scrupulously tidy, and she wasn't. If annoyed, he tended to retreat into silence, while she fired from the hip.

But she had soon settled into the shared intimacies of marriage, realising that these had as much to do with the joint occupation of space as they had with sex.

She had soon grown accustomed to Ross shaving at the bathroom mirror while she was in the bath, and sprawling across the bed, chatting to her as she dressed and put on her make-up. And when she did her hair he would often take the brush from her hand, smoothing the long chestnut strands with almost reverent care, then spoiling the effect altogether by burying his face in the silken, scented mass.

But if she'd thought the honeymoon had taught her everything she needed to know about her new husband, she had soon discovered she was mistaken. That there were areas of his life into which she was not invited.

A couple of times she had overheard him on the telephone, his voice brisk and incisive as he dealt with business matters that clearly had no connection with photography, or the agency. And it had occurred to her that they never really talked about finance, or how he managed to fund that glamorous riverside apartment quite apart from this house.

But when she'd asked, half joking, half in earnest, how many jobs he had, he'd smiled and shrugged.

'Checking that I can afford to support a wife, darling?' he'd countered, which had been no answer at all.

They hadn't been left alone for the duration. After a few tactful days, there'd been visits from neighbouring families, all eager to meet Ross's new wife. All keen to assure her how welcome she was in their community.

And now they would be asked to welcome someone else, she thought, biting her lip.

Another girl would soon walk along the beach hand in hand with Ross, and sleep with him in the comfort of that enormous bed, soothed by the whisper of the sea. A thought that sliced into her heart.

Jenna took off her robe and tossed it across a chair. It was time to stop tormenting herself and get some sleep, she told herself with resolution.

Tomorrow promised to be a day from hell, and she needed to be rested in mind and body in order to cope with its demands.

Of which Ross was only one, she reminded herself.

She lay very still, eyes closed, seeking to empty her mind of disturbing images as she went through the relaxation exercises that someone had once recommended to her for insomnia.

And eventually she found herself drifting slowly down into slumber. But there were dreams waiting for her.

Dreams where she walked alone along an endless beach and her bare feet left no trace of her presence. No trace at all.

When she went downstairs the next morning, she found only Aunt Grace presiding at the breakfast table, lips pursed like the Prophet of Doom.

'Christy's gone into Truro to pick up her wedding dress,' she said. 'And Adrian telephoned.' Ominous pause. 'It seems that the suit fits Ross perfectly.'

The condemned woman ate a hearty breakfast, Jenna thought, accepting the cup of coffee poured for her and reaching for the toast rack.

'Well, that's good news,' she said lightly. 'It saves a lot of trouble for everyone.'

'Good news?' Mrs Penloe stared at her, then shook her head. 'I declare, Jenna, there are times when I cannot understand you.'

And long may that continue, thought Jenna. Or at least for the next thirty-six hours.

Aloud, she said calmly, 'The rehearsal's at four o clock, isn't it? Would you like me to go down to the village hall, presently, and supervise the setting up?'

'Oh, my dear, would you? Mr Sandown means well, but he will insist on using the old trestle tables, and they're really not reliable any more. One of them actually collapsed at the Garden Club coffee morning—the mess was unbelievable. And the caterers have sent a last-minute list of kitchen requirements like the United Nations charter,' she added bitterly. 'So no doubt he'll be grumbling about that, too.'

'Don't worry about a thing, darling.' Jenna helped herself to marmalade. 'I've always been able to handle Mr Sandown. He's a pussy cat. I'll make sure Christy's buffet is on safe legs.'

'Mrs Withers has laundered all the table-cloths, so you'll need to collect them from her,' her aunt mused. 'And then there are the evergreen garlands from the garden centre...'

'I'll do all of it,' Jenna said cheerfully. *Anything—anything to keep my eye on the ball and stop me from thinking.* 'Just make me a list.' She paused. 'Do you want me to hang the garlands as well?'

'Your uncle and Adrian are going to do that,' Mrs Penloe said firmly. 'I don't want you falling off any ladders.'

'The bride's father and the groom being dispensable, of course.' Jenna gave her an affectionate grin, then finished her toast and coffee. 'I'd better get cracking.'

'Thank heaven Christy's an only child,' said her fond mother, rising from the table. 'I don't think I could bear to go through all this again.'

In spite of her best efforts, Jenna was late arriving at the village hall. She had gone to the garden centre first, where, she'd discovered, the garlands with their dark green glossy leaves studded with tiny white and yellow jasmine-like flowers were still being packed in long boxes. And while she'd been waiting for this task to be completed, and the boxes to be placed in the boot of the car, it seemed that everyone who worked there had sought her out for a few words. As she'd known them all for most of her life, she hadn't been able to simply rush away.

But the real delay had come when she'd arrived at Mrs Withers's terraced cottage to collect the table linen. As she'd reached for the gleaming brass knocker the door had been snatched open, and Mrs Withers, minute in a blue-flowered overall, had surveyed her from head to foot, her small dark eyes snapping with mingled pleasure and curiosity.

'Dear life,' had been her greeting. 'So you're back where you belong, and not before time, too.'

An imperious gesture summoned the reluctant Jenna into the cottage and into a spotless living room, bright with polish, where a small fire burned contentedly in the hearth. Before she could protest, she found herself being plied with over-milky tea and home-made biscuits.

'Skin and bone, that's what you are, my little bird,' Mrs Withers commented critically, observing Jenna's ribbed sweater and slim denim-clad hips. 'Comes from fretting, I dare say.'

'Nothing of the sort.' Jenna kept her tone light and upbeat. 'Actually, I'm the ideal weight for my height,' she added, ignoring her hostess's derisive snort. 'And I have a full and busy life in London.'

'London,' Mrs Withers said loftily. 'I went there once. Couldn't abide un.' She added a heaped spoonful of sugar to her cup and stirred it vigorously. 'So you're bridesmaiding Christy Penloe tomorrow. Seems only yesterday you were a bride yourself, with your Ross.'

'Pure coincidence.' Jenna kept her bright smile nailed in place. 'And he's not ''my Ross'' any longer. We're divorced, as I'm sure you know.'

'Then more's the pity. A handsome couple you made, and no mistake.' She paused insinuatingly. 'And now he's back here, too. Funny, that.'

'Pure coincidence.' Jenna said again briskly, draining the last of her tea with a repressed shudder. 'And I'm sure you know the old saying "handsome is as handsome does."'

'I know it.' Mrs Withers nodded fiercely. 'And I also know that a woman without a man is a poor sort of thing. It's been four years and more since I buried Withers, and not a day of it that I haven't missed him cruel.'

It occurred to Jenna that burly Mr Withers with his booming laugh and kind eyes had probably never had an unfaithful thought in the whole of his marriage.

She wanted to cry out, But you don't understand... And bit her lip when she saw the older woman's eyes were sparkling with something other than curiosity.

She said gently, and with real sincerity, 'Well, we can't all be as fortunate as you were, Mrs Withers.' She rose to her feet. 'Now, if I could just have the tablecloths, please? I really do need to get on.'

She laid the plastic bags of snowy linen carefully on the rear seat of the car, and drove off with a final wave.

Once out of sight of the cottage, however, she felt her shoulders drooping slightly. This was the disadvantage of coming back to a place where your life was an open book and thus available for comment, she thought ruefully.

Mr Sandown was the only person waiting for her at the hall, and now he helped her unload the car, complaining in an undertone about his bad back.

'I thought Adrian would be here,' Jenna said, putting the garland boxes into a neat stack.

'So he was,' agreed Mr Sandown. 'He's been knocking in pins round the walls, and some little hooks so all they decorations'll drape nice. But then he went off to fetch something. He'll be back presently.'

'Right.' Jenna consulted her list. 'I'd better start in the kitchen—checking the fridge temperatures for the caterers. Although I can't think why.'

'That'll be Brussels, that will,' her helper said sourly. 'I dunno what they don't want, with their regulations. Separate sinks for washing hands,' he added with scorn. 'My old mother had one sink and she washed everything there, including the six of us children. And what's wrong with that, I'd like to know?'

'Well, it all looks very nice,' Jenna said soothingly, glancing round. The hall had just enjoyed an extensive facelift, with fresh paint everywhere, smart pale green curtains at the high windows, and a new woodblock floor. Christy's wedding reception would be the first major event there since refurbishment.

The kitchen, too, had been set up in a way that would suit even the fussiest hygienist, she decided, crossing those items off her list with satisfaction.

She coaxed Mr Sandown into putting the old trestles back in store and getting out the brand new tables for the buffet, and although he complied with only a token grumble about his deteriorating physical condition, he made it clear he was prepared to do no more.

'Tis time for dinner,' he announced. 'And the missus will have it ready.'

Jenna stifled a grin as she watched him depart. Mrs Sandown's state of readiness, she knew, counted for nothing when compared with the alternative lure of the bar at the Tinners Arms. And she would bet real money on where he was actually heading.

Still, so far, so good, she congratulated herself, glancing at her watch. But time was passing, and if Adrian would only come back they could make a start on the decorations.

She glanced appraisingly up at the walls as she began to remove the garlands carefully from their boxes. The fixings were in place, after all, she mused, and it seemed a pity to wait around indefinitely.

There was a pair of steps leaning against a wall, and she dragged them over to the first window and climbed up, a garland draped over her shoulder.

It was not that easy to hang, she soon discovered. These were big windows, and she could only reach Adrian's hooks by gingerly putting one foot on the narrow sill and stretching at full length, while the elderly steps creaked ominously.

She was glad to find herself back again on *terra firma*, and sorely tempted to leave the rest for someone else to struggle with.

But she'd come here to work, and at least she knew what she was doing now, she thought, man-handling the bulky steps to the next window along and grabbing another garland.

But as she struggled to attach it to its fastening she heard a slithering noise, and felt the ladder began to slide. Glancing down, she realised that the frayed cord which held both halves together had given way, and the damned thing was collapsing on to the floor.

Hastily Jenna snatched her foot away, transferring her entire weight to the inadequate support of the window sill instead, and found herself perched there precariously, on tiptoes, clinging monkey-like to the frame.

Too late, she remembered Aunt Grace's warning, and shuddered, closing her eyes. The strain on her calf muscles was already painful, and her white-knuckled hands couldn't gain any real purchase on the smooth frame. If she took the risk, and jumped backwards, she would land on the ladder and undoubtedly damage herself badly.

Perhaps, she thought, opening her eyes reluctantly, she could manoeuvre herself round and jump sideways. She tensed as she saw that the view from the window had suddenly changed, and that Adrian's car was now parked right outside.

There was no sign of Adrian himself, but he couldn't be too far away. She screamed his name, knowing, as she did so, that he wouldn't hear her through the double glazing. And in order to pound on the glass to attract his at-

tention she would have to let go of the frame.
Which was impossible.

She was close to panic when the hall doors
eventually squeaked open, and cried out again,
'Adrian—help me, for God's sake. I'm slipping.'

She heard running footsteps, the sound of
the ladder being kicked away. Then strong
male hands clamped on her hips, steadying
her, and Ross's voice said tersely, 'Let yourself go, Jenna. Do it now. I'll catch you.'

'I—can't.' Her voice was a whimper, and
she was ashamed.

'Yes,' he said. 'You can. Just relax and slide
down—don't throw yourself. See if you can
get on to your knees. Slowly, now.'

Shakily, gasping for breath, she did as she
was told, lowering herself by degrees, her
hands slipping down the frame. As soon as her
bent knees touched the sill she felt his arms
fasten round her like steel bands, lifting her
back against him. For one endless moment she
seemed to be held there in his arms, and she
felt her whole body clench in a sudden agony
of yearning. Then, at last, she was lowered to
the ground.

Instantly, she wrenched herself free, turning on him. She said between her teeth, 'Don't—touch—me.'

She saw his eyes narrow in disbelief and his mouth tighten. Then he stepped back, raising his hands in a gesture that was almost resigned.

'Well, that has a familiar ring.' His voice was sardonic. 'What was I supposed to do, Jenna? Wait until someone more acceptable turned up? Or let you break your leg and leave Christy to find a substitute bridesmaid as well?'

There was a loaded silence. Jenna felt the throb of tension pulsing between them. Was aware of it building to danger levels and knew she needed to defuse it—and fast.

She stared down at the pattern on the wooden floor. 'I—I didn't mean that as it sounded,' she said at last.

'No?'

'I overreacted, that's all.' Jenna lifted her chin and met his sceptical gaze, her own eyes flashing. 'And I'm sorry. But I was scared—and you—startled me,' she added stiffly.

'I suppose that could be considered an advance on the disgust and contempt I usually inspire in you.' His voice bit. 'Didn't you hear me coming to the rescue?'

She shrugged. 'I saw Adrian's car and thought it was him.' *Relied on it.* She frowned. 'Where is he, anyway?'

'I left him up at Trevarne House. He'll be coming down presently with your uncle. He lent me his car to collect another pair of steps from Thirza's cottage. It was obvious these were going to fall to pieces at any moment.'

'Not to me,' she said. 'Unfortunately. Well—thank you.'

'The pleasure,' he said softly, 'was all mine. But if you're planning any more balancing acts, perhaps you'd save them for when I'm not around. You're not the featherweight you look, and hauling women around wasn't actually part of the treatment my consultant prescribed.'

'Oh, have I interrupted your convalescence?' Jenna clicked her tongue. 'How remiss of me. Especially when you're trying to build up your strength for your next wedding. Or at least the honeymoon part of it.' She paused. 'Have you decided on a suitably romantic location?'

'Of course I could say it's none of your damned business,' Ross said slowly. 'But, as it happens, we may well dispense with the honeymoon.'

'But convention demands it.' Jenna felt as if she was probing an aching tooth. It hurt badly, yet somehow she was unable to stop herself. 'A private time for the newlyweds. You can't deny your bride that.'

'I don't intend to deny her anything,' Ross told her coolly. 'But honeymoons can be over-rated pastimes. I'm already intimately acquainted with my future wife, and she with me, so we don't need a period of seclusion to consummate our vows. I'd prefer us simply to get on with the rest of our lives.'

'And she'll agree with that?'

'Yes,' he said. There was a tenderness in his faint smile that caught at her heart. Caught it—and twisted it in a vice of pure jealousy. 'I'm sure she will.'

Jenna kept her voice even. 'You're really determined to make it work this time—aren't you?'

'Oh, yes,' Ross said quietly. 'You'd better believe it.'

'Yet,' she said, 'if you have this well-nigh perfect relationship, how is it you chose to recuperate from your illness here with Thirza rather than with your fiancée? Or is she not the Florence Nightingale type?'

'I've never asked her,' Ross drawled. 'But she has a lot going on in her life right now, so I decided it would be better this way.'

'And, naturally, you wouldn't want to start off a new relationship from a position of weakness either.'

He shrugged. 'If that's how you want to figure it. I shan't argue with you, Jenna.'

'Nothing new there,' she said tautly. 'The Ross Grantham creed. Never apologise—never explain—never argue. Isn't that how it goes?'

'That may be how it went,' he said. 'But things are very different now.' He paused. 'Do you want to continue this fascinating inquiry into my motivation and philosophy of life, or shall we do something more useful? There are still these garlands to hang up.'

'Just as you wish.' She hunched a shoulder. 'Sure it won't cause a relapse?'

'I'll risk it,' he said. 'But to be on the safe side I'll climb the ladder from now on. I'd hate you to suffer any further mishap. Especially one that might prevent our dance together.'

'Our dance?' Jenna repeated, puzzled, watching him position the new pair of steps, retrieve the garland, and hang it effortlessly. 'What are you talking about?'

He looked down at her as he made a minute adjustment to his handiwork.

'At the reception,' he said. 'The bride dances with the groom. The bridesmaid with the best man. It's one of those conventions you seem so keen on.'

'Well—yes.' *But that was with Tim. I was to have danced with Tim.* She swallowed. 'However, that doesn't apply to us—surely.'

'You'll find it does,' he said, descending to the floor. 'But I'll make it a dance that involves no touching.' His smile was thin-lipped. 'Does that reassure you?'

There was sudden anger in her voice. 'Nothing about you will ever do that. So perhaps we should just—stop talking and work.'

They'd reached the last window when they heard voices and Mr Penloe came in with Adrian. He checked, looking faintly surprised.

'Jenna, my dear. So this is where you've got to.'

'I thought this was where Aunt Grace wanted me.' Jenna handed Ross the final garland, and watched him place it.

'Well, I'm sure it was,' her uncle said. 'But things have changed—become a little fraught. I think Christy would appreciate some support.'

'Then I'll go,' she said. 'We've finished here, anyway.'

'Yes, indeed.' Her uncle looked round, nodding. 'You've done really well.' He paused. 'The pair of you.'

Ross folded the steps and leaned them against the wall. 'We make a good team.' He glanced at Jenna, and she saw mockery in his eyes.

'Yes,' she said. 'But only in the short term.'

His mouth slanted an acknowledgement. As she reached the door his voice followed her. 'Goodbye for the present, Jenna.' A pause. Then, 'See you in church.'

It was safer not to respond in any way. And particularly not to look back at him. Because he might see the tears in her eyes, and that would be a disaster.

*   *   *

She'd regained a measure of control by the time she returned to the house. She found Christy up in her bedroom, surrounded by cases and tissue paper.

'Running away?' she enquired.

'I'd like to,' Christy said with a sigh. 'But only with Adrian. Do you think it's too late to elope?'

'Do that,' Jenna said, 'and I shall follow—and strangle you with a garland of evergreens.' She made a space on the bed and sat down. 'Uncle Henry thought you might need me.'

'I had a little spat with Ma.' Christy looked contrite. 'She was fussing. I asked her not to, and off we went.'

'Well, that was bound to happen eventually,' Jenna soothed. 'Weddings are always stressful.'

'Yours wasn't,' Christy objected. 'I've never seen anyone so calm and composed.'

'I was probably comatose.' Jenna forced a laugh. 'Numbed with horror at the ghastly mistake I was about to make.'

'Garbage,' Christy said roundly.

'Yet that's what everyone thought—including your parents. And in the end, of course, they were proved right. Ross and I did not belong together.'

'Well, I still can't figure out why.' Christy frowned. 'I've never seen two people so in love. Just being round you both was like entering a force field.' She paused. 'Jen, I've never asked before, but what really went wrong?'

'You know what happened.' Jenna picked up a bikini from the bed and studied it as if it was an alien object. 'Ross had an affair with someone from his past—an Australian blonde called Lisa Weston.'

Christy spoke gently. 'I know she was the effect, darling, but what was the cause? Because something must have led to it.'

Jenna shrugged. 'Perhaps, once the novelty wore off, Ross discovered that monogamy bored him.' She hesitated. 'I don't think she was the first.'

Christy was open-mouthed. 'What are you saying?'

'Oh, there were signs, even before the baby.' Jenna bent her head. 'The phone would ring, and no-one would speak when I answered it. I found a woman's handkerchief that wasn't mine in the pocket of his suit, and another time one of his shirts reeking of some expensive scent in the clothes basket.'

Christy frowned again. 'That's not very clever—encouraging your lady-friends to call you at home and bringing home stray bits of laundry into the bargain. Asking for trouble, in fact. Did you ask him to explain?'

'Yes.'

'And?'

'And, naturally, he denied all knowledge of it. He was very convincing. You'd have sworn he was genuinely bewildered. He said he'd probably picked up the hankie somewhere, thinking it was mine.'

'And the shirt?'

Jenna folded the bikini with infinite care and put it in the nearest case. 'He said that girls were always spraying themselves with scent on the tube, and he must have got in the way.'

'So what did you do?'

'I washed the shirt and threw the handkerchief away.'

'And the phone calls?'

'Ross said they were just someone being a nuisance, so he had the number changed and— they stopped.'

Christy was silent for a moment, then she said, 'He could have been telling you the truth, Jen. He was crazy about you. Everyone knew that.'

'Was he?' Jenna stared down at her bare hands. 'If so, it didn't last. It was like a forest fire. It blazed up, and when it died everything was black and empty. No life. No shelter. Nothing.'

She drew a deep breath. 'Whereas with you and Adrian it's the real thing. A sure and steady flame that will burn for the rest of your lives.'

'Oh, Jen.' Christy's voice broke. 'I'm so sorry. I want you to be happy, too.'

'I will be. I am.' Jenna rose to her feet. 'And no one else knows what I've just told you, so please—please keep it to yourself.'

'I promise,' Christy said gently. 'Not even Adrian.' Her brows lifted as Jenna walked to the door.

'Where are you going?'

'I want to find your mother.' Jenna flashed her a quick smile. 'I expect she's just realised that when you and Adrian leave on honeymoon she's going to have an empty nest. Not easy.'

She paused. 'She's probably taken refuge in the greenhouse, as usual. I'll try and tempt her out with food. Will soup and sandwiches do? I feel we should have something. After all, we don't want you fainting at the altar during the rehearsal. And when we've eaten I'll give you a hand with the rest of the packing.'

But once outside the door she made no attempt to go downstairs. Instead, she leaned for a moment against the wall, aware of the uneven thudding of her heart.

What had brought those particular memories bubbling to the surface? she wondered breathlessly. Did she really need such a potent reminder of what a blind, credulous fool Ross had made of her?

I should have confronted him, she thought. Made it clear that I wasn't deceived. But I was scared—scared of losing him—so I wanted to believe him. Needed to think that he was telling the truth.

Whereas in reality I was setting myself up for the biggest betrayal of all.

And each time I look at him—each time I remember the touch of his hands on my skin, and let the ache, the wanting back into my heart and mind—then I'm simply betraying myself all over again.

And I can't do that. At least, not if I'm ever to know another moment's peace.

And she sighed. Because peace might be all that was left for a one-man woman, doomed to spend the rest of her life alone. Without him.

CHAPTER SEVEN

THE tiff between Christy and Mrs Penloe was soon resolved over lunch, and the bride and her mother even enjoyed a little weep in each other's arms while Jenna tactfully took her sandwiches into the garden.

She was glad to have some time to herself. Her last conversation with Christy had disturbed her more than she wanted to admit.

The cupboard door was open, she thought, and all the skeletons were tumbling out.

Because, if she was honest, she and Ross had been having problems long before Lisa Weston came back into his life. Even before the baby...

Almost as soon as the honeymoon was over, in fact.

It had begun when Ross came home one evening to find her poring over a sheaf of estate agents' brochures.

'What are you doing?' He'd looked at her enquiringly, brows raised.

'Doing some preliminary browsing,' Jenna returned airily.

'But we don't need anywhere else to live,' he said quietly. 'We have this flat.'

'Yes, and it's beautiful.' She smiled up at him. 'But it's a bachelor pad, darling. And we need a home. Somewhere we can put down roots. Expand into.'

He said with a touch of grimness, 'I think I need a drink.' He poured himself a single malt, then came to sit beside her. He said, 'Is this a subtle way of telling me that you're pregnant?'

'Of course I'm not.'

He said quietly, 'Well, God be praised for that, anyway.'

Jenna stiffened. 'Would it be such a bad thing?'

'At this stage in the marriage?' His mouth twisted. 'Yes, Jenna, I think it would. We're still learning to live together. We don't need to take on any more commitment just yet.'

'But you're not against the idea in principle?' she persisted.

'I don't know.' His tone was even. 'I haven't thought about it.'

She stared at him. 'But that's why people get married—isn't it? So that they can be a family?'

'Perhaps,' he said. 'But right now I'm more interested in our being a couple. And I thought you liked living here.'

'Yes.' Jenna bit her lip. 'And—no.'

'Ah,' Ross said slowly. 'Care to explain?'

She shrugged evasively. 'I'd like us to be somewhere that's new to us both—and without—resonances.'

He said drily, 'From my past, presumably.' He was silent for a moment. 'If you're waiting for me to apologise for not remaining celibate all these years, then you're going to be disappointed, my sweet. And, yes, other women have shared the bed that we now sleep in. Hell, if it troubles you that much why don't we just buy another bed?'

She said unevenly, 'You find this really funny, don't you?'

'It's becoming rapidly less amusing with every moment that passes.' He swallowed some whisky, the dark face brooding. 'Why did you never mention this before?'

She lifted her chin, 'Because I wasn't your wife before.'

'No,' he said, softly. 'Of course not. You were just another girl sharing my bed—is that it?'

She flushed, furious that he could read her so well.

'Oh, Jenna.' Ross sighed impatiently. 'Can't you see that you were never that? That you are the one—the only one. We don't have to buy a house to prove it. It's our relationship that matters, not bricks and mortar.'

She said, 'I thought you'd want to move, too. Make a fresh start...'

'And I believed we'd just done so.' His tone held a touch of bleakness. He drank the rest of his whisky. 'Do you want to go out to eat?'

She shook her head. 'I'm—not very hungry.'

He stared at her, eyes narrowed.

'Really?' he drawled. 'Then it looks as if I'll have to dine alone. See you later.'

He picked up his jacket, slung it over his shoulder, and sauntered to the door.

As it closed behind him Jenna swept the brochures off the low table to the floor in one furious gesture.

He wouldn't even look at them, she raged inwardly. And, to add insult to injury, he'd walked off and left her without a backward glance. Without even one miserable attempt to persuade her to go with him.

She marched into the kitchen and made herself a self-righteous supper of beans on toast, but it wasn't easy to swallow past the lump in her throat, and she threw half of it away.

Aunt Grace's voice came to her. 'Never attempt to discuss anything serious with a hungry man, my dear.'

Good advice, which she wished she'd remembered at the time.

She was in bed when Ross came home a couple of hours later, lying on her side, facing away from the door. She heard him come into the room and walk softly over to the bed.

She was acutely aware of him standing beside her, looking down at her. Then he said quietly, 'Jenna,' but she made no response, lying without stirring and making herself breathe deeply and regularly.

And presently she heard his footsteps going out of the room again.

She opened her eyes then, feeling slightly foolish and a little sorry, too. She was tempted to go to him in the living room, but that would solve nothing, she told herself. They would only argue again.

No, she would wait until he came to bed, and then pretend to wake up, and turn drowsily into his arms, inviting him to make love to her. And when they were both sated and relaxed, lying entwined in the aftermath of pleasure, she would coax him round to her point of view.

Not something Aunt Grace had ever advised, she thought, smiling into the darkness. But deliciously effective just the same.

She stretched luxuriously, her skin warming at the prospect, then burrowed her cheek into the pillow and waited for him to come to her.

Minutes passed and became half an hour. Turned into a full hour, and then another. Only by that time Jenna was asleep, deeply and genuinely.

When she woke the next morning she was alone, and for a moment she thought he hadn't come to bed at all, but spent the night on the sofa. Except that the rumpled pillow on his side of the bed and the covers thrown back told a different story.

It was very quiet in the flat, so it seemed he had already left for the day. Glancing at the clock on the night table, Jenna saw that he'd allowed her to oversleep, and that she was going to be late for work.

'Hell's bells.' She slid out of bed, grabbing her robe. Coffee, she thought, hot and strong, before her shower.

But Ross hadn't gone to work. He was in the living room, standing silently, a dark silhouette by the sunlit window, looking out at the river.

Jenna skidded to a halt. 'Oh—you're still here. Why didn't you wake me?'

Without turning, he shrugged. 'Because you might still have been playing games.' His voice was flat. 'And this one time I thought I'd allow you to get away with it.'

He paused. 'I've also decided to put this flat on the market, if that's really what it takes to make you happy. Find a house you like, and I'll set the wheels in motion.'

'Oh, Ross—darling.' She would have run to him, but there was something about the set of his shoulders that warned her she might be risking a rebuff, and she hesitated, huddling her robe around her because she felt suddenly cold.

She said, 'But you have to like it, too.'

'This is your game, Jenna, with your own rules. I choose not to play.' He turned and looked at her, the dark face unyielding, his eyes remote. 'But understand this. From now on, you never again pretend to be asleep, or have a headache, or lie about the time of the month, or any of those other shabby little tricks. Our marriage is worth more than that.'

She bit her lip. 'Ross—I...'

'There's coffee in the pot,' he went on as if she hadn't spoken. 'I'll see you tonight.'

She stood once more, watching him walk away from her. Wanting to call him back, yet not making a sound. Realising she'd won. But feeling as if somehow she'd lost.

She threw away the brochures that had sparked off the disagreement, feeling that they were somehow tainted—even unlucky. She wanted to begin her house hunting with a clean sheet. Then laughed at herself for being superstitious.

She did her sums carefully, calculating how much the flat would fetch, and the amount of mortgage they could afford, especially if she had to give up work for any reason and they were reduced to just one income, she thought with a private joyous smile.

At the same time it occurred to her that she had little real idea how much Ross earned, although he clearly liked to live well.

I suppose this is something we should have talked over before we got married, she thought, wrinkling her nose ruefully.

It was certainly something they ought to discuss before she started contacting estate agents in earnest. Although, because of the events of the past eight hours, she probably needed to postpone her enquiries to a more appropriate time.

But when Ross came home that evening, the cool, taciturn man who had departed that morning might never have existed. He swept in, smiling, his arms full of champagne and long-stemmed crimson roses.

'I was a bear—forgive me,' he whispered passionately as he picked her up and swung her round, his mouth warm and hungry on hers. 'Nothing matters but being with you.'

Jenna yielded thankfully, gloriously, as he carried her into the bedroom. 'Love me.' Her voice was husky. 'Ross—love me always, and I won't ask for anything else.'

'You have it.' His hands were tense with desire as they stripped the clothing from her body. There was no time for indulging in tender preliminaries. Their mutual need was too strong, too fierce for anything but immediate satisfaction. As he entered her Jenna cried out, her voice thick with passion. She was aware of nothing but the heat of him filling her, making her complete, and she gave with total recklessness, her body twisting beneath his with unthinking sensuality as she drove towards culmination.

At the height, Ross made her wait for a trembling eternity, then gave her the release she craved, making her body fragment into rapture.

Later, lying entwined, they drank champagne, and Ross poured some of the chilled wine over her breasts, licking every last drop of it from her nipples before beginning the slow, sensuous ascent to pleasure again.

Afterwards, 'If this is making up, maybe we should argue more often,' he murmured, a note of laughter in his voice.

'No.' Jenna was vehement as she nestled closer to him. 'I hated arguing. I've been miserable all day.' She took a deep breath. 'Ross—I've had time to think, too, and we don't need to move anywhere else—not yet. We can wait—save some money first.'

He tipped up her chin so he could look into her eyes. 'Why do you say that?'

'I was thinking this might not be a good time. After all—this flat must have cost a fortune, and there's the upkeep on the Brittany house as well.'

'It's not a problem.' He kissed her mouth gently. 'Have your house, Jenna. I want you to be happy.'

'But I wanted somewhere with a garden—and they're asking ridiculous prices.' She sighed. 'We couldn't afford anything like that.'

'Yes,' he said quietly. 'Actually, we could.'

Jenna stared up at him. 'I don't understand…'

'That's entirely my fault,' he said. 'There are things I should have told you before this. I suppose I was waiting for the right moment, and this seems to be it.' He paused. 'You see, the house in Brittany wasn't my only legacy. My other grandfather also made me his heir, and he left me money—quite a lot of it. Some of it's tied up in trusts, of course, but the rest is available if and when I want to use it. Only I never have before.'

Jenna saw his mouth tighten with remembered pain, and put up a hand to stroke his cheek. 'Why not?'

'Because of the trouble it's always caused.' He sighed. 'Even when I was a small child. I can remember the friction between my father and Grandpa Grantham. He was a financier, and expected his son to follow in his footsteps—become a solid citizen. And that was never going to happen.

'Instead he found himself having to bail him out over and over again, until at last he decided that enough was enough. For a long time there was no contact between them, although Thirza did a lot to heal the breach. She was tough and sensible, and Grandpa recognised that. But, all the same, he made it brutally clear that Dad would never see another penny of his money, or take his place on the bank's board. And that he'd made a new will in my favour, bypassing him completely.'

Jenna gasped. 'And he actually did so?'

'Oh, yes,' Ross said drily. 'And I can't altogether blame him for that. Dad's track record with money did not bear scrutiny. But it created a rift between my father and myself that I've always regretted. Dad was full of resentment and treated me as if I was some kind of robber baron, although we were reconciled before he died—again, thanks to Thirza.

'So, from the first, the money was a burden. And I was sufficiently my father's son to want to go my own way and leave my seat on the board empty, although there's been a certain amount of pressure on me lately to think again.' He pulled her closer, his mouth warm on her skin. 'Perhaps they think marriage has tamed me.'

'How wrong can they be?' Jenna returned breathlessly, feeling the blood leap in her veins.

'They may see my using the money as a concession in itself.'

'You'd rather we didn't...?'

'It's not that.' Ross was silent for a moment. 'I'm always aware of how much trouble it's caused in the past. I don't want it to affect what we have.'

'It won't.' Jenna drew his head down and kissed his mouth. 'It's just a way of finding the home of our dreams, that's all.' She moved against him, softly and sensuously, revelling in his instant response. 'Oh, darling, we're going to be so very happy. And nothing will ever spoil that.'

Even at this distance, the memory of those words—and the wild, unthinking optimism which had inspired them—had the power to make Jenna shiver, as if a cloud had suddenly obscured the brightness of the sun.

Was it really the money? she asked herself with a kind of despair. Did it cast some kind of blight—start the rot? If we'd stayed in the flat would our relationship have been different? Could it have survived?

She got up from the garden seat and walked back towards the house. No, she thought. That was just a fantasy. The reality was Ross being exactly what he'd said—his father's son—restless and unfaithful.

And nothing could survive that.

Over the next few hours she threw herself almost grimly into preparations for the wedding. There was certainly plenty to do. Other family members and friends would start arriving soon, and every bedroom at Trevarne would be in use, so Jenna found herself flying around with armfuls of sheets, blankets and towels under her aunt's direction.

Some of the guests would be staying at the Fisherman's Arms, or in bed and breakfast accommodation in the village. And for the final few, mostly young and male, there would be air mattresses and sleeping bags in quiet corners of the house.

'I hope they'll be comfortable,' Christy said, her forehead creased anxiously as she stuffed yet another pillow into its case.

'Of course they will,' Jenna returned robustly. 'Besides, it's only for one night.'

'Yes.' Christy hesitated awkwardly. 'Jen—I know I should have mentioned this before, but I hope you didn't mind my not inviting Natasha. I know that you're close—flatmates and now business partners—but the guest list was getting out of hand...'

'And, anyway, you've never been her greatest admirer,' Jenna supplied drily.

'Oh.' Christy pulled a face. 'You guessed.'

'I've watched you bending over backwards to be polite and friendly,' Jenna admitted, amused. 'That's usually a bad sign. But don't give it another thought, love. I'm sure it never occurred to Tasha that you'd ask her.'

'I expect it did.' Christy's tone was almost waspish. 'Not a lot gets past that one.'

Jenna decided it was best to ignore that. Christy didn't realise just what a tower of strength Natasha had proved over the past months.

'It's just as well she's not here.' She shook her head. 'I can imagine how she'd have reacted to Ross's presence.'

'Yes,' Christy said thoughtfully. 'So can I.' She paused, sending Jenna an odd glance. 'Are you going to tell her?'

'Naturally. And how I weathered the storm.' Jenna lifted her chin. 'She'll be proud of me.'

'Will she?' Christy shrugged. 'Well, you know her better than I do.' She glanced at her watch. 'Hell, we'd better get changed. It's nearly time. See you downstairs in fifteen minutes?'

'Yes.' Jenna's smile was so wooden her lips had splinters. 'Yes, of course.'

No matter how hard she'd worked, the prospect of the wedding rehearsal had been there all day in her consciousness, like a high wall on an obstacle course.

She was half tempted to go as she was, in washed denim jeans and a sweater, but the vicar was a conventional man, who specialised in pained looks, and finding herself on the receiving end of one of them would only draw attention to her. When what she really wanted was to be invisible.

She'd brought a dress to wear, in her favourite green with a tight bodice and a swirl of a skirt, but that had been when the best man was a stranger, for whom she was prepared to make an effort.

She didn't want Ross to imagine, even for a moment, that she'd dressed to please him.

Unobtrusive was the name of the game, she told herself, sorting restlessly through the clothes she'd brought with her and coming up with a cream linen skirt and a matching round-necked sweater in fine wool.

She pushed her feet into a pair of low-heeled bronze pumps and studied herself in the mirror with dissatisfaction. The shadows under her eyes had deepened, and her entire facial bone structure looked gaunt and haggard.

I look like a ghost, she thought. Or, worse, a woman in mourning.

Grimacing, she got to work with the concealer, then applied a dusting of blusher and a touch of brownish lip colour.

On the stairs, she met Aunt Grace, who was staying behind from the rehearsal to welcome arriving guests.

'Putting a brave face on it all, dear?' She was inspected rapidly and given an approving pat. 'I'm sure that's wise. I was just coming to find you. You're wanted on the phone.'

Jenna frowned as she continued down to the hall. She hadn't been expecting any calls, but, then, she hadn't been anticipating any of the other things that had befallen her at this wedding either, she reminded herself with a certain tension.

She picked up the receiver. 'Hello?' For a moment there was no response, just an eerie, almost deafening silence, reminding her of all those other unexplained silences. She found she was gripping the carved edge of the telephone table.

She said harshly, 'Who the hell is this? Who's there?'

There was a crackle, then Natasha's voice said, 'Jenna—is that you?'

'Oh, Tasha.' Jenna let out a gasp of relief, then paused. 'What's the matter? Has something gone wrong at the gallery?'

'No—no, everything's fine. But I suddenly found I was thinking about you, and wondering how things were at the wedding of the year?' Even at this distance Jenna could pick up the faint edge in Natasha's voice. 'Is Christy still planning to go through with it, or has she had second thoughts?'

'Christy has never been happier,' Jenna returned with emphasis. 'And the weather is glorious. It should be a wonderful day.'

'And you're coping all right?'

Jenna bit her lip. The correct response, she knew, was, Never better, and that was what she should say, but this was her concerned friend, so why pretend?

She said slowly, 'Not really. When I arrived I found Ross was here.'

'Ross?' She could feel the shock waves reverberating down the phone. 'Is this some kind of sick joke?' Natasha's tone sounded harsh, almost aggressive.'

'Unfortunately, no.' Jenna kept her own voice temperate. 'He's staying with Thirza while he gets over some virus.'

'Did you know about this in advance?' Natasha demanded harshly.

'No, of course not.'

'But you've seen him?'

Jenna sighed soundlessly. 'I haven't had a great deal of choice. He's had to step in as best man.' She swallowed. 'It's—just one of those things.'

'My God—after all you've been through, you're still letting them do this to you. I cannot believe it.' Natasha paused. 'I knew it. I sensed you were in trouble.' Her voice quietened, became more persuasive. 'Jenna, listen to me. Get out of there—now. You don't need to be treated like this. Tell them all to go to hell, and come back to London.'

'I can't do that. It would upset everyone and everything. And, besides, it's not as bad as it sounds. Ross and I have declared a truce.'

'A truce?' Her friend's laugh was shrill. 'You'll be telling me next you've decided to forgive and forget. Or maybe you've already done so.'

Jenna bit her lip. 'No, but we've agreed to try and behave decently to each other for the duration of the wedding.'

'Decently?' Natasha echoed derisively. 'Are you crazy? Ross is incapable of decency. Has it slipped your mind that he deserted you after your miscarriage? That he proved over and over again that he was nothing but a serial womaniser? Someone who discarded his lovers like soiled clothing—and that you were no exception?'

'No.' Jenna's voice shook. 'I remember everything that happened, including a lot of stuff that I must have buried in the back of my mind and hoped I would never discover again. Only seeing Ross again has brought it all to the surface.'

'What kind of thing?' Natasha asked sharply. 'What are you talking about?'

'It doesn't matter, because I'm dealing with it.'

'Of course it matters. I can't bear to think of you torturing yourself like this. You've got to tell me...'

'Tasha, I really can't discuss it now. It's the wedding rehearsal, and they're waiting for me.'

'Will Ross be at this rehearsal?'

'Naturally. I told you—he's acting as best man.'

'And your family are allowing this?' Natasha gave an angry laugh. 'My God, they should be shielding you from him.'

'They don't have to, because there's nothing left between Ross and me.' Jenna hesitated. 'And anyway, he's getting married again.'

This time the silence was so profound she thought they'd been cut off.

She said, puzzled, 'Tasha—are you there?'

'Yes,' Natasha said. 'Yes, of course.' She laughed again, an odd, strained sound. 'Ross—does not learn from his mistakes, does he?'

Jenna winced, but kept her voice light. 'Apparently it's the real thing this time.' She caught sight of Christy signalling to her from the front door, and stiffened. 'Look, I must go. We'll talk when I get back, but I'm fine—really. See you soon.'

It was a relief to put the phone down. Sometimes Natasha carried her protectiveness too far, she thought unhappily as she went out to the car. At times during the conversation she'd sounded almost paranoid.

And, far from blaming Christy for failing to invite her to the wedding, Jenna felt almost grateful to her cousin for the omission.

As for herself—only twenty-four hours to go and she would be free again. And safe.

She waited with Christy outside the church while Uncle Henry went in to make sure everything was ready for the rehearsal to begin.

'He's even arranged for the organist to be there so that we can practise walking up the aisle without falling over,' Christy said, leaning against the side of the car and squinting up at the sun. She sighed. 'The way things are going I shall probably be making the trip on my knees anyway.' She paused. 'You haven't got a cigarette on you, by any chance?'

'No,' Jenna said calmly. 'Because I don't smoke, and nor do you.'

She grinned at her cousin. 'Do I detect a touch of bridal nerves at last?'

Christy shook her head. 'Oh, Jen, it's all so chancy. People get married, but they don't seem to stay married any more. And I don't want us to become another statistic.'

Jenna shrugged. 'Tell me about it.'

'Oh, *hell*.' Christy gave her a rueful look. 'Me and my big mouth. But I swear I wasn't having a dig.'

'I never thought you were. But, if it's any consolation, you and Adrian have looked like a couple from the moment you met. And you're both the product of stable marriages, which they say helps, too.'

Christy smiled reflectively. 'I once asked Ma if she'd ever thought about divorcing Pops, and she said absolutely not—but she'd contemplated murder a few times. I can settle for that.'

And they were both laughing when Mr Penloe came out to summon them into the church.

It was an ancient building, constructed on a site where, it was believed, far more primitive forms of worship had once been conducted. Jenna sometimes found it dark, but today, with the afternoon sun pouring through the windows, dappling the stone floor with pools of colour, and the elderly pews already decorated with lovers' knots in primrose and white ribbons, its dignified beauty was at its best.

As the stately notes of the 'Wedding March' filled the air, Christy walked slowly forward on her father's arm, with Jenna pacing behind them. Tomorrow she would have flowers to carry, but for now she kept her hands clasped in front of her to hide the fact that they were shaking.

Because this was all too reminiscent of everything she needed so badly to forget. Like a slow-motion replay of her own wedding, she thought, her heart thudding unevenly. Except that this time she was cast in a minor role.

Ahead of her she could see the kindly figure of the vicar waiting at the chancel steps. She realised that two tall figures were rising from the front pew and moving to join him. And that they'd both turned to watch the small procession making its way up the aisle. Adrian's face was one broad grin of delight as he saw them approach, but his companion was unsmiling, pale, even gaunt beneath his tan. And he was looking only at Jenna.

Don't look back at him, she told herself, her throat tightening uncontrollably. Look at the back of Christy's head, the vicar, or the cross on the altar. Anywhere but at him...

And yet, as if mesmerised, her gaze was drawn inexorably to his.

It was like being plunged into a furnace, she thought, her steps faltering involuntarily.

Because, in Ross's eyes, she saw anger, bitterness and naked pain. And, transcending all these, a stark and passionate physical hunger that sent her mind and senses reeling out of their strictly imposed control.

You can't—you can't do this to me! The words were screaming silently in her head as she tried and failed to tear her eyes from his. As she felt, shocked, the harsh, pagan stir of her blood in a response as terrifying as it was inevitable.

She realised that Christy was turning to her, pretending to hand her a non-existent bouquet, but passing her, instead, the keys to her car.

And at the same time she became sharply, agonisingly aware that Ross had taken a step nearer to her. That if he put out a hand he could touch her.

Panic rose inside her like nausea. Her hand closed round the keys—the miraculous, life-saving keys—as she took one pace back, and then another. Until she whirled round and fled down the aisle, ignoring the startled voices calling out to her, out into the sunshine and the waiting car.

And escape.

CHAPTER EIGHT

SHE was in no fit state to drive, but she drove all the same, away from the church, away from the village, away from the fool she'd just made of herself. That—that most of all.

She had an abiding inner vision of all those astonished, appalled faces watching her go. And Ross, alone unmoving and unmoved, like a pillar of granite, observing this act of total self-betrayal.

She took a corner too fast and too wide, and a car coming in the opposite direction blared its horn at her, shocking her back to reality.

That was all she needed, she castigated herself. To end up in pieces physically as well as emotionally. Besides, she was going to be in quite enough trouble with Christy as it was. She didn't need to bend her car as well.

She drove on more sedately, hugging the tall hedges for safety, her hands clamped on the wheel as if it was her last hold on sanity, then took a turning totally at random, heading for the ever-present coast.

Here the landscape was wilder and more bleak, with the wind shivering over rocks and clumps of gorse and whining in the ruins of a long abandoned tin mine.

Straight ahead of her the Atlantic heaved itself at the guardian cliffs, then fell back defeated.

Jenna parked a safe distance from the edge, then grabbed the stray fleece Christy had left on the rear seat, huddling it around her against the chill of the strong breeze as she left the car. She stood for a moment, catching her breath, then made her way to a flat boulder and sat down.

To her relief, there was no one else around. She needed to be alone and out of reach for a while, as she sorted out in her mind what had just happened. Because there was every chance that she was going to cry, quite loudly and quite bitterly, and for that she didn't require an audience.

There was no sound but the eternal wash of the ocean, and suddenly the solitary cry of a bird—a curlew, perhaps—sparking an answering wrench of loneliness deep in her gut.

She tucked her trembling hands into the sleeves of the fleece and bent forward, staring sightlessly at the rutted ground at her feet.

It wasn't the anger in Ross that had defeated her and put her to flight, but that searing glimpse of fierce, almost anguished desire.

Because he had no right to look at her like that, his dark gaze stripping away her clothing for his own private satisfaction.

So many times before she'd encountered that particular expression in his eyes—that focussed, almost stark sensuality, combining heated demand with passionate promise.

She would look away, feeling a responsive warmth invade her skin, a swift scald of excitement building within her. Knowing that by the time they were alone together she would be sobbing, half-frantic for him. Which had always been his intention.

There was never time for subtlety or love play. That would come later. There was only the fever of their breathing as they wrenched their clothing apart, desperate for the graze of skin against bare skin. For the mutual filling of their senses.

And afterwards they would sleep, sated, in each other's arms, his hand possessively cupping her breast.

A shudder of pure sensation quivered through her at the memory.

But it wasn't just the pleasure of sex which had enthralled her, binding her to him for ever, although she acknowledged that had been a potent force.

Jenna remembered, too, the laughter, the tenderness, the private jokes, the way he'd reach for her hand as they walked along the street, all the small day-to-day intimacies of a relationship, made all the more poignant because she'd been robbed of them so swiftly and cruelly.

Oh, God, why couldn't she have been enough for him, as he'd been for her?

And why had she been too blind to realise that he was turning away from her?

One last time she would allow herself to ask those questions for which she had never been able to find the answers. Always before she had pushed them away, knowing that she would find such self-interrogation too painful to deal with.

But now she was already suffering more than she could bear, and it was time to examine the failure of her marriage once and for all time.

Not that it would be easy. It would be like trying to piece together the fragments of a treasured piece of crystal that she knew was smashed beyond repair, and that would leave her fingers cut and bleeding.

Yet she owed it to herself to find an explanation. To understand why she had lost him. And, most important of all, to justify her decision to cut him out of her life.

Maybe once this unfinished business had been dealt with she would finally be able to forget.

She lifted her head and stared at the restless, tumbling sea.

She had never wanted to regard herself as any kind of victim, but all the same she had always been certain in her own mind that she was the injured party, and Ross was solely to blame for their divorce.

But over the last few days she'd been faced with the unpleasing fact that others might not totally share her view. Even Christy, who'd always been one of her staunchest supporters.

And this was what she now had to confront. Because simply repeating to herself that Ross had been unfaithful to her because he was his father's son didn't work for her any longer.

When had things started to change between them? she asked herself, biting her lip. Was it when they'd moved into the tall house in Notting Hill she'd found for them, with its spacious rooms and stripped floorboards, and, importantly, the lawned garden at the rear shaded by a magnolia tree?

Jenna had had a secret vision of herself, sitting on a rug under the tree watching her baby kicking happily in the sunlight, and hugged it to herself smiling.

On a more practical level, there had been four bedrooms, two bathrooms, and a brand-new kitchen, so they'd been able to move in right away without needing to carry out any preliminary work.

'There's even a basement which you could convert into a dark room,' she told Ross, bubbling. 'You're going to love it.'

Ross kissed her smiling lips. 'I love you,' he told her softly. 'And that applies wherever we may happen to live.'

Thirza was one of their first visitors. 'My word,' she said with a touch of dryness. 'Playing house, Jenna?'

Jenna, who'd been given free rein with the furnishings, too, and was pleased with her efforts, stiffened. 'Don't you like it?'

'What's not to like?' Thirza looked round again. 'It's—quite charming, if a little large.' She paused. 'So, which room is going to be the nursery?'

Jenna flushed. 'It's far too soon to be thinking of that,' she said, ignoring the fact that she'd already decided on the sunny rear room on the second floor.

'Quite right,' said Thirza. 'Two being company and all that.' She gave Jenna a pleasant smile. 'Is that coffee I smell?'

But Natasha's reaction had compensated for Thirza's lukewarm response.

'It's absolutely perfect. A dream house,' she said. 'You are clever, darling. And it will hold its resale value,' she added practically.

Jenna laughed. 'We're never going to sell,' she said. 'Or at least not until the children are grown-up and gone.'

Natasha's head snapped round. 'Children?' The word was almost shrill. 'Surely you're not pregnant already?'

'Not as far as I know.' Jenna gave her a surprised look. 'But is there some reason I shouldn't be?'

Natasha hesitated. 'None at all.' She gave a smiling shrug. 'I just can't visualise Ross coping with nappies and broken nights, that's all.'

'Nonsense,' Jenna said. 'He'll be a wonderful father.' *Once he gets used to the idea.*

Which, she had to admit, he showed no signs of doing. He was preoccupied more with the agency, frankly unhappy with the quality of the work being sent back. Clearly chafing that he wasn't still in the front line himself.

'You wouldn't go back, would you?' Jenna asked one night as they lay in bed together.

'Would it be so terrible?' He was playing with her hair, twining it round his fingers, brushing it across his lips.

'I don't know.' She tried to speak lightly. 'How terrible is danger?'

He sighed. 'Jenna, I could leave the house tomorrow and be run over by a bus. Or walk into a terrorist bomb. You can't rely on staying safe—not any more.'

'But you don't have to take unnecessary risks either.' She was on full alert, her heart thumping. 'And you're making a great job of running the agency. Everyone says so.'

'Really?' His tone was sardonic. 'Yet I feel as if I've been on an overlong holiday, stranded in some pleasant, undemanding limbo, and it's time to get back to some real work.' He sighed, briefly and sharply, then tipped up her face and kissed her. 'But we won't talk any more about it now. Let's get some sleep.'

He slept, but Jenna did not. She lay awake, staring into the darkness, her mind full of explosions and falling buildings, and the wailing of people in pain and distress. And Ross would be there in the front line—in the thick of it all.

Her throat closed in panic. How could he even think of going back, when he was married—when he had a life with her?

She would have to give him, she thought, a good reason to stay.

In the morning, after he'd left for work, Jenna buried her foil strip of contraceptive pills deep in the garbage sack she was putting out for collection. She wasn't proud of herself, but desperate circumstances called for desperate measures.

Six weeks later, a pregnancy testing kit told her that her ploy had worked.

She left the gallery early, and shopped for a special meal. Flowers, she thought, and wine and candles. The works.

When Ross came home his brows lifted at the sight of the shining dinner table laid for two.

'Are we celebrating something?' he asked. 'Don't tell me I've forgotten some monthi-versary?'

'No, nothing like that.' She put a basket of warm toast for the pâté on the table. 'I've had some good news, that's all.'

He was very still for a moment, his eyes narrowing as he studied her, then he said lightly, 'You've been promoted—given a pay rise—discovered some new artist who's going to take the world by storm? All of these?'

'None of them.' She filled the wine glasses. 'I'll tell you after we've eaten.'

'No,' he said, and his voice was suddenly steely. 'You'll tell me now, Jenna.'

She'd practised the words in her head all day—the perfect phrase that would be not too blunt, but not coy either.

But what she heard herself say was, 'I'm pregnant.'

She looked at him, waiting—wanting to see joy explode in his face. Expecting to be snatched up into his arms.

Instead, his head went back, and he looked at her as if she was a stranger. He said quietly, 'But that's impossible. Because we've talked about this. We agreed. And you're on the pill.'

She took a step towards him. Put out her hand. 'But nothing's one hundred per cent reliable. You know that.' She touched the tip of her tongue to her dry mouth. 'I—I had a slight tummy upset a few weeks ago. That can affect things.'

'Did you?' he said. 'How unfeeling of me not to have noticed. Now, I'd have said you hadn't had a day's illness since we met.'

She hugged her arms round her body. It was all going terribly wrong, and she had no idea how to retrieve the situation. Or even if she could…

She tried again. 'Ross, I thought you'd be pleased.'

'Oh, no, Jenna,' he said, too softly. 'You know better than that. And that's exactly why you've forced my hand like this. Bad move, my love.'

He picked up his jacket and walked to the door.

'Where are you going?'

'Out,' he said. 'To think, and probably get very drunk.'

'But I've cooked this lovely meal...'

'Then it's just as well you're eating for two, darling,' he said. 'Isn't it?'

And a moment later she heard the door slam behind him.

She cleared the table, threw away all the careful preparations, then went to bed and cried herself to sleep.

She awoke very early the next morning, and lay for a moment, wondering why. Then two things occurred to her. Firstly, that the bed beside her was still empty. And, secondly, that she was about to be violently sick.

She only just made it to the bathroom. And when, at last, she raised her head groggily from the toilet bowl Ross was there, pale and unshaven, but concerned.

'Where—where have you been?' Her voice was a croak.

'I slept on the sofa.'

He wiped her face with a damp towel, then lifted her into his arms and carried her gently back to bed.

'Would you like some tea?'

Jenna shuddered violently. 'Just some fizzy water, I think.'

'Probably wise.' He paused, then bent and kissed her. His lips were tender, offering reconciliation, and perhaps acceptance.

'Well, you've had the dream, darling,' he whispered wryly. 'Now welcome to the reality.'

That particular reality, Jenna recalled without pleasure, had impinged on her with monotonous regularity over the next two months. The up-side had been that within half an hour she'd felt fine and bursting with energy again, so the nausea, although unpleasant, hadn't caused any major inconvenience.

She hadn't been able to wait to tell everyone, travelling down to Cornwall for the purpose. Her family had been delighted, but clearly surprised.

'A baby—and so soon in the first year,' Aunt Grace pondered, after she'd hugged her niece. 'Can you really afford it?'

'Of course. I'm going to work until the last minute, and Ross is incredibly well paid at the agency. And I told you about his inheritance...'

'Oh,' said Aunt Grace. 'I wasn't actually thinking about money.'

Thirza had received the information quietly, and without any astonishment.

'And how does Ross feel about this?' she asked. 'Coping with the inevitable, I suppose.'

Jenna lifted her chin. 'He's thrilled to bits.'

In truth, she wasn't altogether sure how Ross was dealing with the prospect of fatherhood. He could not have been kinder and more protective. But she was nevertheless aware that his concern was for her rather than the tiny life growing inside her.

He'll feel differently when it starts to show—and to move, she thought, placing a hand over her still-flat abdomen.

He was also beginning to suggest with increasing frequency that she should give up work, and for the life of her she couldn't understand why.

'Darling, I'm fine,' she assured him. 'And I'd be so bored at home, alone all day. Surely you can understand that?'

'Yes,' he said slowly. 'But, just the same, I think you need to take extra care.' He gave her a taut smile. 'You look—tired sometimes.'

She went into his arms, hugging him close. 'But I really enjoy my work,' she murmured. 'And I've never felt better in my life. Besides, Mr Haville and Natasha keep me wrapped in cotton wool.'

It was no more than the truth. She'd been hesitant about breaking the news of the baby to Natasha, as she hadn't been sure what her reaction would be. But there'd been no need to worry. Rather to her surprise, Tasha had been over the moon, and had fussed round her solicitously ever since. Indeed, right up to the moment when...

Jenna's hands gripped the rock on either side of her. Now she was coming to it—to the terrible, unbelievable thing that had befallen her. The memory she had tried unavailingly to push away ever since.

It had begun like any other day. At the gallery they'd been planning another exhibition, and there had been a stack of canvases up in the office, waiting to go to the framers.

Jenna's offer to help carry them downstairs had been turned down flatly by Natasha. 'I wouldn't dream of it,' she declared. 'You shouldn't be lifting heavy weights, and those stairs are lethal anyway.'

'They're not heavy, just bulky,' Jenna protested. 'And, anyway, I'm not made of glass.'

Natasha paused. 'All right then,' she allowed grudgingly. 'We'll do it between us. But you only carry one at a time.'

It was on Jenna's third trip that it happened. She waited at the top of the stairs for Natasha, who was coming up, then began to descend carefully. But as she reached the fourth step she suddenly lost her footing. She cried out and clutched at the rail, but she was already falling forward, her body rebounding helplessly from step to step, until she reached the wooden floor at the bottom of the steep flight. And the painful pit of darkness that awaited her there.

She learned afterwards that the ambulance had been there within minutes, but she was already bleeding when she arrived at the hospital, and miscarriage had proved inevitable.

She lay in the narrow bed in a private room, physically bruised and emotionally torn into pieces. Yet, oddly, unable to cry.

They'd called it 'an unlucky accident' and 'no one's fault', but Jenna knew better, and blamed herself. After all, she was the one who'd wanted this pregnancy—who'd manipulated it into being, ignoring Ross's wishes. And now she was being punished. Taught in one poignant lesson that it was dangerous to engineer life to suit one's own wishes, because fate could and would hit back.

And her agonised heart grieved for the tiny being she had lost.

'These things happen,' one of the nurses told her, trying to be kind. 'But as soon as the consultant gives you the all-clear you can try again.'

'No,' Jenna said. 'I won't be doing that.'

The woman gave her a bracing smile. 'Your husband may have a point of view on that, dear.'

'Yes,' Jenna said with difficulty. 'I—I'm sure he will.'

And she turned painfully on to her side and faced the wall.

The medication they'd given her allowed her to sleep, and when she woke Ross was there, sitting beside the bed, white-faced and hollow-eyed.

He said, 'I was out of the office and they couldn't find me. Not at once.'

He took her hand and lifted it to his cheek, cradling it there. 'Oh, darling.' His voice broke. 'You could have been killed.'

'No,' she said. 'The baby died instead. In my place.'

'Oh, my love,' he said. 'My love. I'm so sorry.'

'Why?' She shook her head, her eyes almost blank. 'You never wanted this baby. You knew I'd tricked you into it. Didn't you?'

'Yes,' he said. 'But that doesn't matter. It stopped mattering a long time ago. You must believe that.'

'Must I?' She sighed. 'Somehow it doesn't seem very important any more.'

'It's important to me.' Ross paused. 'Can you remember how it happened?'

'I tripped on the stairs. Or slipped. Whatever.' She removed her hand from his clasp. 'It's ironic, isn't it? You wanted me to give up work, but I couldn't. And if I had, I'd still be having the baby.'

'Darling,' he said. 'Don't think about that now.'

'No,' she said. 'There's no point. Because it's all over.' She was silent for a moment. 'Will you tell everyone—my family—and Thirza? And ask them not to fuss. Apparently it happens a lot—with first babies.' She smiled at him politely, almost apologetically. 'And often it's for the best. They said that, too.'

'Oh God,' he said. 'Jenna—*Jenna*.'

A nurse came bustling in, saying it was time Mrs Grantham got some more sleep and that he should come back in the morning.

Ross looked at her coldly. 'I'd like to stay with my wife.'

'No,' Jenna said. 'There's no point. Please go. I—I'm very tired.'

For a moment he looked as if he was going to protest. Then he sighed. 'Very well,' he said, and his voice was infinitely weary. 'If that's what you wish...'

She was kept in for a couple of days, with the small room filling up with flowers and loving, anxious messages. She was also offered grief counselling, but declined.

Mr Haville came to see her, wringing his hands and saying he'd examined every inch of the stairs and could see no reason for her fall— no reason at all.

Later, Natasha arrived, looking pinched and white. 'I can't believe it,' she kept saying. 'I just can't believe it. I keep seeing you lying there, not moving.' She shuddered, then paused. 'Do you remember how it happened?'

'No, it's all pretty much a blank.' Jenna paused. 'I was carrying a canvas, wasn't I? Did it survive?'

Natasha pulled a face. 'Not really, but that's the last thing you should be bothering about. You just need to get strong again.'

Jenna found she needed all the strength she possessed when the time came for her to go home. She sat beside Ross in the passenger seat of the car, taut as a drum, as they drove back to the house. The hospital room had become a refuge, but now she was out in the cold world again.

'Darling.' Ross was watching her, worried. 'Will you be all right? I need to get back to the agency. Something's come up. But Christy's coming over to be with you.'

'Thank you,' she said. 'However, there was really no need.' She summoned a smile. 'I'll be fine—really.'

But she wasn't fine at all. Suddenly the house was like an empty shell, sterile and heartless, where her footsteps rang hollow on the polished boards.

Up in the would-have-been nursery, the pretty chest of drawers she'd bought only a couple of weeks before had gone, and the paint cards and swatches of fabric had also been removed. Making it just another room again.

This had to be Ross's doing, and she knew she should be grateful, yet a blind, unreasoning anger began to stir in her. How easily he'd disposed of all her hopes and plans, she thought. Proving how little they'd meant to him.

The sound of the doorbell was a relief, and Christy's warm and comforting presence a blessing.

As they sat in the kitchen drinking the coffee her cousin had made Jenna said, 'Ross has stripped the nursery. Everything's gone.'

Christy laid a hand over hers. 'I'm sure he's done it for the best,' she said gently. 'He's very concerned about you.'

'Yes.' Jenna looked down at the table. 'But he doesn't really care about the baby. He never did.'

'Oh, Jen, I'm sure you're wrong.'

'Not one word of regret.' Jenna bit her lip hard. 'Not one. He's hardly mentioned...'

'It can't be easy for him either,' Christy soothed her.

'No?' Jenna asked harshly. 'Isn't that why he cleared out the room? What's the old saying—"Out of sight, out of mind"? Everything back to normal as soon as possible?'

'Perhaps it's his way of dealing with it—the only way he knows.' Christy patted her hand. 'Don't be too hard on him, love.' She rose. 'Do you feel up to a trip down to the Gate for some food shopping? I'll put a casserole in the oven for you for tonight.'

'Aren't you going to stay and have some?'

'Not tonight. I think you two should be alone and do some talking. Besides, I have a date.'

'Oh.' Jenna managed a smile. 'Anyone nice?'

Christy said slowly, 'I think he might be. His name's Adrian, and he works for a merchant bank. But it's too soon to judge.'

'Yes,' Jenna said tautly. 'Because there's another old saying—"Marry in haste, repent at leisure."' She nodded almost fiercely. 'Don't you make that mistake.' And thought, *As I did...*

Ross looked tired and preoccupied when he came home that night, and it was clearly no time for a heart to heart. In fact he said little, apart from enquiring how she felt, praising Christy's casserole, and asking if there was anything she wanted to watch on television.

Jenna went up to bed first, and Ross followed half an hour later. She was propped up on her pillow reading when he came into the room.

As he began to unbutton his shirt she said, quickly and breathlessly, 'Ross, the consultant said I should get as much rest as possible.'

'Of course,' he said. 'For a start, I've contacted a domestic help agency and they're sending someone in the morning.'

'I—I didn't mean that.' She swallowed. 'I really need to get a good night's sleep—without being disturbed.'

Ross was very still for a moment, then he tossed his discarded shirt over a chair and began to unbuckle his belt. 'Meaning?'

'Meaning I've made up a bed for you in the next room.' She forced a nervous smile. 'Just for a few nights.'

'I see.' He was silent for a moment. When he spoke again his voice was level, but there was an underlying note of harshness. 'Jenna, I need to sleep with you—to hold you. But that's all. You surely don't think I'm so crazed with lust that I'd force myself on you sexually? I'm your husband, not a monster.'

'That's not what I'm trying to say at all.' She sat up, pushing her hair back with a defensive hand. 'I just want the chance of a peaceful night's sleep for a little while. Is that so much to ask?'

'Peace,' he said slowly, 'is a commodity in pretty short supply these days. And I'm not sure this is the way to achieve it. But if you don't want me in your bed, I won't insist.' His mouth twisted sardonically. 'And I'd better not kiss you goodnight either—just in case that arouses the brute in me. So—sweet dreams, my love.'

The door closed behind him and Jenna was alone, which was just what she'd wanted, so it was stupid to feel so desolate. And galling to find that she couldn't sleep anyway. She was still too bruised and sore to toss and turn, so all she could do was lie there in the darkness—and endure.

She found herself wondering whether Ross was finding sleep equally elusive. She could always find out, of course. He was only a few yards away on the other side of the wall, and the temptation to go to him—to feel the welcoming warmth of his arms enclosing her, soothing her, was almost overwhelming.

Almost, she thought unhappily, but not quite. Because nothing between them could ever be the same again, and it was useless to pretend otherwise. However much she might want him physically, emotionally they were on different planets, and she was going to need time to come to terms with that.

Gradually her bruises faded, and she began to heal mentally as well as physically. But she and Ross were as far apart as ever, by day as well as night. And the more time passed, the harder it became for her to invite him back into the bedroom they'd once shared.

She realised she was hoping he'd ease matters by making the first move. But he didn't, and she was almost glad when the Penloes invited her down to Cornwall to stay with them.

'Ross says you're still pale, and not eating properly,' Aunt Grace told her on the phone. She paused. 'It's a shame he can't come with you.'

'Oh, well,' Jenna said lightly. 'He'll be all the more pleased to see me when I come back.'

But when her week's cosseting was over, and she returned to London, it was to discover that Ross had given up his desk job and was about to depart on another assignment abroad, thus damning any hopes she'd cherished of a blissful reconciliation.

'You didn't think to discuss it with me first?' She stood helplessly, watching him pack.

He shrugged. 'It's my career—my life, Jenna,' he told her quietly. 'And we rarely discuss very much at all these days. But when I come back we'll talk, if you want.'

She said hoarsely, 'I can't believe that you're doing this. Leaving me on my own after—after what happened.'

His mouth tightened. 'You're not on your own, my sweet. You never have been.' He ticked off on his fingers. 'You have your family, friends, offers of counselling—a whole support system. Including your job at the gallery, which you're about to return to. I doubt very much if you'll notice my absence.'

She wanted very much to plead. To cling to him and beg him not to go. But her pride wouldn't allow that.

He hadn't wanted the baby, she thought, pain closing in on her. And now, it seemed, he didn't want her either.

She, however, missed him achingly, every hour of every day. And when he returned he found the spare bed stripped and his clothes and belongings back in the marital bedroom, in mute acknowledgement that his exile was over.

But even that didn't work out as she'd hoped. When he made love to her she was tense and anxious, and he was almost icily restrained.

At the end, he said bleakly, 'I'm sorry,' and turned away from her. While he slept she lay awake beside him, tears of bewilderment and disappointment squeezing under her eyelids. All her worst fears confirmed. She found herself remembering some anonymous phone calls when they'd first moved in, and other mysteries too—and wondering.

And there was another potent reason why she couldn't relax in his arms. Although the obstetrician had given her the all-clear, she was actually scared of becoming pregnant again. Of displeasing Ross by conceiving another unwanted baby.

Eventually, on the occasions when they did make love, it was swift and almost perfunctory, as if fulfilling some unappealing obligation.

Once she had dreaded him going away, but now it was almost a relief. Or that was what she told herself. But at the same time she was weeping inside, watching her life collapse around her, and bewildered by the speed at which it seemed to be happening.

It was the sudden escalation in the Middle Eastern conflict he'd been sent to cover that finally brought her to her senses. The knowledge that his life was seriously in danger made her realise she wasn't prepared to allow her marriage to slide away, out of control. She had to make a stand.

She watched the television news channels almost obsessively, as well as ringing the agency every day to demand if there'd been any contact with him, only to be disappointed.

But she mustn't worry, they told her. Ross would come out of it all right. He led a charmed life.

But nothing could reassure her. By day she paced the house, unable to concentrate on anything but the next newscast and grim reports of spiralling violence. At night she lay curled into a foetal position, with his favourite sweater wrapped round her.

And when the agency called her, at long last, to tell her they'd heard from him, and that he and another group of journalists and photographers were already flying back, she sat for a long time with the phone cradled against her breasts, tears of relief pouring down her face.

Then she moved into action—filling the house with flowers, making sure the fridge was packed with his favourite food and wine, and putting clean sheets on the bed before setting off to the airport to meet him. Something she hadn't done before.

This time, she told herself, she was leaving nothing to chance. And when she walked into his arms he would know that everything had changed.

His flight had landed when she got there, and she roamed Arrivals like an animal in a cage, mouth dry, palms damp, her eyes restlessly scanning the doorway through which he would emerge.

He was one of the last to come through, and as Jenna saw him she raised a hand to wave—to attract his attention and bring him to her. Then froze as she realised what she was seeing.

He was walking slowly, his head bent, and he was not alone. A woman was walking beside him, slim, young and blonde, and his arm was round her shoulders.

As Jenna watched, shocked and helpless, she saw the girl pause and her arms go up round Ross's neck, drawing him down to her in a long, lingering kiss, her body pressed against his with total familiarity.

Dispelling, once and for all, any last, desperate hope she might have had that their closeness was that of colleagues who'd just shared a common danger.

Jenna heard herself make a sound—hoarse, almost visceral. And then she was turning, running like a hunted creature through the crowd to the exit, intent only on flight. Seeing nothing but the intimacy of the embrace she had just witnessed. Hearing nothing but the rasp of her breathing and her voice silently moaning her husband's name.

CHAPTER NINE

JENNA had been at home for over two hours when Ross returned. Two hours in which her imagination had run riot as she'd visualised Ross and his blonde entwined in some hotel room.

She heard the cab draw up outside, and his key in the door, then the sound of his bags being deposited in the hall. But he did not call out her name, and her throat tightened in fear as well as anger.

And when, a moment later, he came into the drawing room, and saw her standing rigidly by the empty fireplace, he made no attempt to go to her. Instead, he remained by the door, the dark face enigmatic as he watched her in a silence that seemed to echo round the world.

At last she said, 'I—came to meet you at the airport.'

'Yes,' he said, his mouth twisting faintly. 'I thought I saw you—disappearing.'

She threw back her head. 'Who is she, Ross? Your blonde—companion.'

'Her name is Lisa Weston.' His voice was even. 'She's an Australian journalist and she works for the *Sunday Globe*.'

'And is that all you have to tell me about her?'

'I thought,' he said, 'that you'd have worked out the rest for yourself.'

Her lips parted in a soundless gasp. She'd expected him to deny it, to come up with some explanation. Some reassurance. She realised how desperately she'd been relying on this.

She said hoarsely, 'You've been—sleeping with her?'

'Sleep,' he said, 'didn't feature highly on the agenda.'

The brutality of it sent her reeling mentally, as if he had raised his hand and struck her across the face.

She stared at him, searching his face for some sign of softening—some remorse. A touch of regret. Something she could use, even now, to build a bridge between them. But the cool mask was impenetrable. Merciless.

She whispered, 'How could you? Oh, God, *how could you*?'

'Because she wanted me, Jenna.' His voice seared her to the bone. 'And that made a refreshing change, believe me.'

Her legs were shaking under her. Her mind was shuddering into denial, telling herself that this was the man she loved—the man who'd taught her to want him to the point of oblivion. The man she'd planned with such excitement to welcome home again into her heart and her arms.

And who could not be saying these things to her.

She was dying inside, but she managed to find a voice from somewhere.

She said, coldly and clearly, 'Then maybe you should make the change a permanent one.'

His brows lifted. 'Of course, if that's what you wish.' He paused. 'Have I time to pack the rest of my things, or would you prefer me to leave at once?'

He sounded polite, even matter of fact. He might have been asking if she wanted some coffee, Jenna thought incredulously. She stiffened, her nails digging viciously into the palms of her hands.

'Yes,' she said. 'Please go—now.'

She couldn't bear, she thought, for him to glimpse all the pathetic arrangements she'd made to please him. To signal that she wanted them to make a fresh start together. And that she'd hoped, stupidly, innocently, that their reconciliation would begin in bed.

She turned away, staring down blindly at the cold hearth. Even now, she realised in stunned disbelief, she was still waiting for him to speak her name—to step across the abyss that divided them and come to her. To hold her while he apologised. While he offered some kind of excuse for his betrayal of their marriage and begged for her forgiveness. While he told her that the pressure they'd all been under had driven him momentarily crazy...

Tell me anything, she thought, anguished, and I'll cling to it like a drowning man to a rope.

But there was nothing. Just the sound of his footsteps receding into the hall. And then the door closing behind him as it had done so often before. Only this time it was for ever.

The anger which had sustained her went with him, leaving a vacuum into which pain began to pour in suffocating waves.

And she sank down on to her knees, her numbed lips repeating, 'It's over. It's all over,' again and again, as if it was some mantra that she relied on for her ultimate salvation.

So, she had done it. She had confronted her most agonising memories. But had she managed to exorcise the demons that had stalked her ever since? Could she now, sanely and rationally, put the past behind her?

Because she had to face the fact that, in spite of what he had done,

Ross was still there, entrenched in her heart and mind. Whereas he had moved on. Found another woman—another life.

The irony was that she'd been telling herself constantly over the past few days that once the wedding was over she would never have to see him again. Now she was faced with precisely that situation and it was wrenching her apart. Repeating, all over again, the agony of betrayal—of desertion.

And what kind of a fool does that make me? she asked herself, shivering.

Even now she wasn't sure how she'd survived the days immediately following Ross's departure. Her anger had carried her along as

she'd packed up his clothes and other posses-
sions, erasing every trace of him. And before
she'd closed the last bag she'd placed inside,
on top of everything else, so it was the first
thing he would see, the small velvet case con-
taining her wedding ring. And then she'd put
it in the hall with the other bags and boxes to
await collection. Giving him, she had told herself, no excuse to linger.

But he hadn't needed any excuse. In the end
he'd removed his things while she was at
work, leaving his key on the hall table as a
sign that their separation was complete and he
would not be returning.

But, all the same, acting on Natasha's advice, she'd had the locks changed.

Over the next weeks she had begun to discover what loneliness meant. The house on
which she'd pinned so many hopes had become just another piece of real estate, cold and
without heart. She'd hardly been able to bear
to spend any time there, remembering what
used to be. And mourning for what might have
been.

Without Ross, she thought, her life had become soulless and meaningless, and she might
have drifted for ever but for Natasha, who'd

found her a divorce lawyer, and an estate agent, and urged her forward into her new single life.

She'd been a wonderful friend, of course, but Jenna had wished sometimes that she wouldn't be quite so obsessively vitriolic about Ross. She'd felt quite raw enough without having his sins detailed to her on a daily basis.

I wonder why she dislikes him so, she thought, with a little sigh, then paused as the sound of an approaching car engine alerted her to the fact that she was no longer alone. That she was going to have to share her sanctuary. But it was time she was leaving anyway, she acknowledged, rising reluctantly from her rock. Time she went back to Trevarne House and grovelled to Christy for messing up the wedding rehearsal.

She turned to walk back to the car, and paused, dismayed, as she realised the vehicle parked next to it seemed all too familiar.

Oh, God, she thought, swallowing. It's Thirza's Alfa Romeo.

Not only that, but Ross and Adrian were climbing out of it and walking towards her, both of them unsmiling.

Jenna stood her ground, her chin lifted defiantly. 'Hi,' she greeted them with an assumption of nonchalance. 'Come to enjoy the view?'

'On the contrary, I see very little to admire,' Ross returned harshly. He held out his hand. 'I'll have Christy's keys, if you don't mind. Adrian's going to drive her car back.'

She hesitated, suddenly wary. 'Then I'll go with him.'

'No,' he said. 'You're staying with me. Because it's time we talked. Got a few things out into the open.'

'And if I don't want to?'

'You have no choice in the matter.' His tone was brusque. 'And we've wasted quite enough time searching for you as it is. So hand over the keys, unless you want me to shake them out of you.'

For a moment Jenna considered defiance, then, as their eyes met and she read the purpose in his gaze, she decided discretion was best.

'How very macho of you.' Reluctantly she produced the keys and dropped them into Adrian's waiting hand. 'And I thought you were supposed to be convalescing. You seem to have made a lightning recovery from your mysterious illness.'

He shrugged, the dark eyes still hard. 'It's astonishing what effect a few days' serious aggravation can have on the constitution.'

'Well, fortunately for both of us, it won't last much longer,' she said tautly. She turned to Adrian. 'Is Christy very angry with me?'

'You know better than that,' Adrian said quietly. 'She's—concerned.'

'That I'll spoil the actual ceremony by running off in front of everyone?' Jenna shook her head. 'I shan't.' She tried a smile. 'You know what they say—bad dress rehearsal, good performance.'

'So they tell me.' Adrian turned and began walking towards Christy's car. 'See you both later.'

'Adrian.' Jenna started after him. 'Please, take me with you...'

But Ross caught her easily, his arm going round her like an iron bar, preventing any further attempt at flight. 'Don't you listen?' he asked coldly. 'I said you were going with me.'

'Leave me alone, damn you.' She struggled unavailingly to free herself, realising with disbelief that Adrian was driving off, apparently deaf and blind to her predicament. 'I'm going nowhere with you.'

'You're planning to walk back to Trevarne?' Ross shook his head as he released her. 'I don't think so. Which doesn't leave you many options, unless you intend to jump off the cliff. Now, there's a thought,' he added mockingly. 'Why don't we jump together? They could call this place ''Lovers' Leap'' and run bus tours out here.'

'We are not lovers.' Her voice shook. 'And I mean to keep my feet firmly on the ground. Anyway, you wouldn't jump,' she added defiantly. 'In spite of the risks you've always taken in your work, you're not the suicidal type.'

'No,' he said softly. 'I have a strong sense of self-preservation. Yet there have been plenty of moments in the past couple of years when I'd have happily opened a vein.'

Their eyes met, and Jenna felt her skin shiver, as if his hand had brushed her, as she encountered the intensity of his gaze.

'But not any more,' she said, recovering rapidly. She adopted a mocking tone of her own. 'Not when you have so much to live for.'

'Why, yes.' His smile was cool. 'Off with the old and on with the new. I can recommend it.'

'Is that all you came here to say?'

'It isn't even part of it.' His hand closed on her arm. 'Let's go for a walk.'

She wrenched herself away. 'I can manage that without help.' Her voice was mutinous. 'You don't need to touch me.'

'Don't I?' The dark brows lifted. 'Perhaps that's something we should include in our discussion.'

'I don't think so.' She looked past him, suddenly not wanting to meet his gaze, aware that her pulses had quickened. 'Just say what you have to and get it over with,' she added curtly. 'I should be getting back to Trevarne. Christy might be needing me.'

'Oh, you're all heart,' Ross said gently. 'Was it Christy you were thinking about when you did your spectacular runner a short while ago?'

'I shall apologise to her for that, naturally.' Jenna took a firm grip on her dignity. 'I—I had a panic attack. It—happens.'

'All you had to do was follow your cousin up the aisle and stand there.' He paused. 'Not too onerous.'

She glared at him. 'The circumstances were—unusual, to say the least.'

'For both of us,' he acknowledged, his mouth twisting. 'Yet I managed to stand my ground.'

'Yes,' she said. 'But you don't have my memories.'

'Of course not,' he said softly. 'You are Jenna the victim, Jenna the vulnerable, Jenna the fragile flower. Don't you think you're rather over-playing that particular role, my sweet, and it's time for a change?'

'You—bastard.' Her voice was thick. 'I wasn't the one who was unfaithful.'

'Not in the conventional sense, perhaps,' he came back at her harshly. 'But you stopped being a wife long before I had a mistress. And you know it.'

She came to a halt, turning on him, her eyes blazing. 'What the hell are you saying?' Her voice rose. 'That somehow it was all *my* fault?'

'No,' Ross said, unmoved by her surge of anger. 'But it wasn't all mine either. It takes two to make a marriage, and two to break it.

And that's what we need to talk about, before it's too late.'

She hauled herself back under control. Managed a shrug. 'Too late has come and gone. We're divorced.' She took a breath. 'So none of this actually matters any more.'

'No?' he said. 'Then if it's all so unimportant why did you run away this afternoon? And why have you been dancing around me like a cat on hot bricks since our first meeting?'

'I—I don't know what you're talking about.' It was a feeble response at best.

'Stop playing games,' Ross said harshly. 'And try to be honest. You ran away today because you were suddenly confronted by a truth you couldn't deal with, and that has to stop if there's any hope for us.'

She said breathlessly. 'Us? There is no "us". And I'd like to go back to Trevarne, right now.'

'I'm sure,' he said. 'But it's not going to happen, Jenna. Not until we've looked at our marriage and established where it went wrong. And that wasn't during my brief fling with Lisa, either,' he added harshly. 'The rot had set in long before that. Even before you shut me out of your life when you lost the baby.'

'The baby you didn't want,' she threw at him.

He was white under his tan, his mouth a compressed line. When he spoke his voice was like ice. Ice that burned. 'Don't ever say that to me again, Jenna. I admit that the news of your pregnancy wasn't the most welcome I'd ever had, but that was because I already knew I'd be going back on the front line, and it was an extra responsibility I didn't need right then. Also, I didn't appreciate the way I'd been manipulated into it,' he added bitingly. 'Suddenly love and laughter had been translated into house and baby, whether I was ready for that or not. And I had no say in the matter. You were determined to conceive, at all costs, and I was presented with a *fait accompli*.'

He paused. 'But I couldn't stay angry for long, Jenna, and you must have known that. You were far too precious to me. And so was the child we'd made together. Because I realised that was just another part of the love and laughter that I treasured so deeply. God, I cared so much that I wanted to keep you safe and cherished for the whole nine months. I'd even have had the baby for you, if I could.'

He shook his head. 'When you had the miscarriage I felt as if the sun had gone out for ever, but I knew what you were suffering, and that I had to be strong for you. Or that's what I was told on all sides. But it never seemed to occur to you, or anyone, that I could be hurting, too. That I would have given my soul to weep and have the comfort of your arms around me.'

He took a breath, his face stark—remote. 'Instead, you didn't want me anywhere near you. I wasn't even allowed in your bed, but banished to another room.'

She was trembling. 'The consultant...'

'To hell with that,' he said roughly. 'I talked to him, too, remember. He said that you'd need love to help you through the grieving process. He took it for granted that would be mutual, and unstinting. He also said that once you'd recovered, we should try for another baby.

'But the wall you built between us, Jenna, wasn't just bricks and plaster. It was an emotional barricade with no way through for me. So you stayed in your private world and I was left to mourn alone. Have you any idea how hard—how bloody impossible—that was?'

She said 'I—I didn't know—I didn't realise...'

'You didn't ask,' he returned, more gently.
'And I began to wonder if you even cared.
Whether you'd ever really wanted a husband
at all, in the fullest sense of the word—or just
someone to father your children and provide a
roof of your choosing for them.'

Her head went back in shock. 'That's—unfair.'

'Perhaps,' he said. 'But you don't think very
clearly when your life is falling apart. When
the wonderful shining girl that you love has
become an aloof stranger who only permits sex
on sufferance.'

He sighed sharply. 'In many ways, snipers
and bombs seemed easier to deal with.'

She drew a deep, painful breath. 'And Lisa
Weston?'

'She was kind,' he said. 'At a time when
kindness seemed like a forgotten dream. And
when I was lonely, and scared witless most of
the time, although I'm not offering that as an
excuse.

'We talked one night—when, admittedly,
I'd had too much to drink—and we ended up
in bed. That was it, and that was all of it.

Afterwards the guilt cut in, and the self-hatred, because I'd used her, and it didn't solve a thing and never would.'

She swallowed. 'Are you telling me that— it only happened once?'

'Yes,' he said. 'Although that makes it no better. It was still weak, selfish and unpardonable.'

She said in a low voice, 'Ross, I—I can't believe you're telling me the truth. Don't forget I saw you together, and it clearly wasn't over for her.'

Ross's mouth tautened. 'No,' he said slowly. 'I don't think it was. And that was another good reason to feel guilty—to hate myself. Because, as I'd always known, there was only one woman in my life that I would ever want and need, and I resolved that when I got back to London I wouldn't leave again until I'd put things right between us. Until I'd persuaded you that our life together was worth saving.

'Only you came to meet me at the airport,' he added quietly. 'And I knew then that you'd seen me saying goodbye to Lisa. And that I'd ruined everything. Taken the dream we had, and smashed it.'

Jenna stared down at the ground. 'It didn't look like goodbye,' she said in a low voice. 'And you went to her after you left me.'

'No,' he said. 'I did not. I went to a hotel for a couple of nights, and then I moved in with Seb Lithgow while I got a flat sorted out. But there was never any question of being with Lisa. I didn't feel that way about her, God forgive me.'

She began, 'But I was told…' then paused awkwardly.

He said softly, 'I wonder by whom? Or could I hazard a guess that it was your best friend and business partner?'

Jenna flushed. 'She meant it for the best. She told me about a rumour she'd heard, because she didn't want it to reach me from anyone else.'

Ross's mouth twisted cynically. 'Now, that I do believe,' he drawled.

She bit her lip. 'You've never had any time for Natasha,' she accused.

He shrugged. 'That cuts both ways.'

'She's always been there for me. I don't know what I would have done without her.'

'You might still be married.'

The shock of that held her mute for a moment. She said hoarsely,

'What is that supposed to mean?'

He was also silent. Then he said, 'I don't imagine she was upset when we split, or that she did anything to bring about a reconciliation.'

Jenna tilted her chin, ignoring an inner suspicion that this was not what he'd originally meant to say. 'She was never your greatest admirer. You're right about that.'

'And wrong about everything else?' he queried softly. 'Is that what you're saying?' He paused, his eyes fixed on hers gravely, searchingly. 'That panic attack, for instance, Jenna? Let's get back to that for a minute. What inspired that, I wonder?'

'I don't want to discuss it.' She made a play of looking at her watch. 'I really should get back. We have a houseful of people...'

'And your aunt can't cope without you, naturally.' His tone was sardonic. 'It won't work, Jenna. I promised myself I wouldn't let you run out on me again.'

She sank her teeth into her lower lip. She said hoarsely, 'What—what do you want from me? Absolution? All right—you have it.' She swallowed. 'I'll even admit that I was to blame, too. I see that now. I—I've made myself look back at everything that happened between us—and it was a shock. Because I realised I didn't like myself very much—not the self-absorbed, obsessive creature I was then. Thirza once accused me of playing house, and I hated her for it, but I think she was right.'

She paused. 'No one could have been sweeter to me than Uncle Henry and Aunt Grace, but they weren't my real parents. They were lost to me, and I think what I was trying to do was recreate them in ourselves—the father, the mother, the loved child.'

She tried to smile and failed. 'The perfect set-up. Only it was all a fantasy. It had nothing to do with us, or our marriage, and it's taken me all this time and all those tears to see that. And later I—I was too caught up in my own misery to think what you might be enduring. And I shouldn't have shut you out. Driven you away as I did. It was stupid—and cruel. And I was duly punished for it, as I deserved to be.'

She spread her hands helplessly. 'So, there you have it. Now—will you let me go?'

He was smiling. 'Not a chance, my love.'

'What else can I say? What would satisfy you?'

He said with sudden roughness, 'To hear you tell me that you love me, that you always have done and you always will. That every minute we've spent apart has been a living nightmare. And that when you saw me in church today you realised that, in spite of everything, we still want each other as desperately as ever. And that's what scared you. That's why you ran.'

She was shaking. 'Ross—don't do this to me. To either of us. We—we're not the same people any more...'

'That's what I'm counting on.' He turned her to face him, his hands gripping her arms, his face intense. 'We got married, my darling, because nothing could keep us apart. But that wasn't enough. We both had things to learn—about ourselves, and each other—and we learned them in the hardest possible way, and were almost destroyed in the process. But now we have another chance, and it's not going to pass us by. I won't let that happen. Because I need you, Jenna, like I need food to eat and air to breathe.'

He shook his head. 'In a way, going down with that virus was a blessing in disguise, because it gave me time to think, instead of racing round the world, using work to blot out the past, as I'd been doing. There were moments in the hospital when the treatment wasn't working, and it wasn't certain that I was going to survive. I realised then that I didn't care. That life without you was no life at all. And I swore that if I recovered I would get you back somehow.

'And that's why I decided to stay on, even when I discovered I'd be around for Christy's wedding. Because I knew it would bring you, too, that I'd eventually get a chance to talk to you—discover if you still cared, even a little.'

'Oh, I care,' she said unevenly. 'I just didn't realise how much. But I didn't want to admit it.'

'You fought me every step of the way,' he said. 'I tried needling you—making you jealous—and you brushed me aside every time. I was almost beginning to despair. Until I saw you in church today, walking towards me, and I remembered how you looked on our wedding day, my beautiful wife. And I wanted you so much it nearly tore me apart.

'And in that moment, like a lightning flash, I saw you wanting me, too. And when you turned and ran it actually gave me hope. Because you were admitting that you knew it wasn't over between us. And that a dozen divorces couldn't alter the way we still feel about each other. Now, deny it if you can,' he added passionately. 'And if you do I swear I'll walk away and never trouble you again.'

The tears that she'd managed to dam back for so long began to trickle down her white face.

'Ross—if that's how you feel, why did you let the divorce go through? Why didn't you come to me—ask me to think again—give our marriage another chance?'

'Because I knew how badly I must have hurt you,' he said. 'And I was ashamed. Besides,' he added drily, 'it seemed as if you couldn't wait to be rid of me, which confirmed all my worst fears -that you'd actually stopped loving me long before I'd been unfaithful.' He paused. 'If I had come to you, what would you have said?'

'I—I don't know.'

'Then maybe we needed a breathing space,' he said quietly. 'Time to reflect and get our priorities sorted out. To reach a stage where we could let our love for each other heal the wounds of the past.'

She was suddenly very still. 'But you have other priorities, Ross. You said so. You're planning to get married again. You can't just—cut her out of your life.'

'I've no intention of doing so.' He reached into his jacket pocket and took out a small jeweller's box. 'Remember this?'

Jenna swallowed. 'My wedding ring? You mean—the woman you were talking about—that you were going to marry—was me?'

He nodded. 'No one else. Give me your hand, my love.' When she obeyed, he slid the gold band back on to her finger. 'Will you marry me, Jenna?' he asked in a low voice. 'Will you now, at last, be my wife, and the mother of my children? I swear I'll never betray your trust in me again.'

'And I promise I'll never again turn away from you,' Jenna whispered, and lifted her face for his kiss.

At first he was gentle, as if her lips were the petals of a flower he was afraid to bruise, and then, as she responded with unguarded, passionate ardour, he cast his own restraint aside, kissing her with all the pent-up hunger that the long months apart had engendered.

His hands were shaking as they explored her body, pushing aside the fleece and sliding under her thin sweater to find the warm swell of her breasts, to stroke the hardening peaks into a glory of erotic pleasure. And she sighed her delight and longing against his mouth.

Her starved body was coming to life again under his caress, melting and burning as his touch became more intimate, more demanding. The long fingers traced a familiar, sweet path down her spine to her flanks, then pulled her to him, his hands on her hips, so that their bodies ground together. Making her know, beyond question, how deeply and hotly he was aroused. And how completely she was desired.

She swayed in his arms in a kind of sensuous intoxication, her mouth a heated seduction under his, her hands as seeking and as urgent.

She would have given herself to him there and then. Would have sunk down to the short windswept turf, drawing him after her.

But Ross pulled himself away from her, with a sound between a groan and a laugh, standing with his hands on her shoulders as he recovered his breath.

His eyes swept her face, lingering on the fever-bright eyes, the flushed cheeks and parted, faintly swollen lips. He said unsteadily, 'I think it's time we went home.'

'But where can we go?' Jenna's voice was husky. 'What are they all going to say if we show up together.'

'If Adrian's done his work well, they'll have said most of it already.' He took her hand, tugging her back towards the car. 'And, anyway, I only care about you.'

She hung back. 'Darling, maybe we should wait—for each other—until we get back to London.'

'No way,' Ross said firmly. 'I've never been a fan of cold showers, and I'm damned if I'm going through the next twenty-four hours with this kind of ache in my guts. We've both spent too many lonely nights already, my love. But that ends right now.'

'Yes, Ross.' Her voice was demure, but the look she sent him combined mischief and passion in a mixture that quickened his breathing.

She expected him to drive back to Trevarne House, but instead he stopped outside Thirza's cottage.

'Oh, God,' Jenna said, appalled. 'Ross—we can't. She never approved of your marrying me in the first place. You know that. She'll be furious…'

'Have a little faith,' Ross said, as he took her up the path. 'You may get a surprise…'

They found Thirza in the sitting room, sitting beside a crackling log fire and studying a book on ancient embroidery.

She glanced up, her brows rising questioningly as she looked from one to the other.

Ross said quietly, 'Thirza—I've brought my wife home with me.'

'This time to stay, I hope,' his stepmother said with a touch of her old austerity. 'If you've both decided to stop behaving like fools.'

Jenna gave an unsteady laugh. 'I think we have.'

'I'm delighted to hear it.' Thirza got up briskly from her chair. 'Well, Grace has invited me to dinner at Trevarne tonight. I'll make your excuses, shall I?'

'Please.' Jenna nodded, feeling suddenly absurdly shy.

'And as your bedroom won't be occupied I think I'll spend the night there,' Thirza added meditatively. On her way to the door, she patted Jenna's flushed cheek. 'You'll find a spare pillow in the linen cupboard, my dear, if you need it. But I dare say you'll make do with one.'

At the door, she paused, looking back at them.

'And bless you both,' she said. And went out, leaving them alone together.

CHAPTER TEN

THEY went up the narrow stairs hand in hand, past the linen cupboard where the spare pillow would wait in vain, and into the long, low room at the back with the wide bed under its snowy quilt.

In many ways, Jenna thought, it was like their first time together. She stood, shaking, as he undressed her, his face absorbed, his hands and mouth magically gentle as he adored each inch of skin that he uncovered.

'Oh, God.' His voice was ragged when she was finally naked. 'You're so lovely.'

Jenna looked into his eyes and saw his hunger for her. Saw too that it had made him vulnerable—even a little uncertain.

She reached up, pulling his head down to the sudden fierceness of her kiss. 'Then love me!'

Their bodies were fierce, too, as they rose and fell, entwined and urgent, their mutual need driving them on. Later there would be time for tenderness, but now there was shallow hectic breathing, and little feral cries. There was the rasp of sweat-dampened skin, and the cling of mouths that had been starved of kisses for too long. There was a burning compulsion to possess and be possessed, and thereby to transcend all known heights.

There was a sheer physicality that was also spiritual.

There was a yielding and a taking that somehow became one and the same. And at the end, before they were even aware, there was a soaring, almost brutal rapture that left them drained, half weeping in each other's arms.

'I love you,' Ross said hoarsely, when he could speak. 'God, but I love you.'

'Oh, Ross—oh, darling.' She was weeping, partly from joy, partly from the depth of sensual fulfilment she had just experienced. 'I'm sorry. So sorry. All the time we've wasted...'

'Hey, now.' Ross tipped up her face, wiping away the tears with a gentle hand. 'We're together now, and that's all that matters. Isn't it?'

'Yes,' she said. 'That's all.'

He said, 'I also think, my sweet, that we have to stop beating ourselves up over the past. Because we can't change a thing.'

'I know that,' she said. She kissed his shoulder. 'I'm so happy that it scares me. Because in my heart I don't feel I deserve it.'

'You mustn't say that, my love. Perhaps we didn't treat each other very well, but we'll do better in the future.'

He kissed her slowly and very thoroughly. 'I told you once that I wasn't going to make the same mistakes again,' he murmured. 'And I meant it. But I'll make others, and so will you, and we'll have rows, and shout and bang doors. But we'll also remember how very nearly we lost each other, and that will be our salvation.'

She said, 'I'm sorry I cut my hair. I know you hate it.'

'Actually, I think it suits you.' He brushed a few damps strands away from her forehead. 'It was the reason why you had it cut that I hated.' He paused. 'On my way back, that morning, I went into the hairdresser's and persuaded her to give me a long strand of it as a keepsake.'

'Stella did that?' Jenna propped herself up on an elbow. 'What on earth must she have thought?'

'At first that I'd escaped from somewhere. Then I explained, and she melted.' Ross stretched luxuriously. 'Tell me, Mrs Grantham, are you hungry?'

'I suppose I should say, "Only for you, beloved",' Jenna said ruefully. 'But the truth is I'm starving.'

Ross grinned at her and threw back the covers. 'So am I. Let's eat.'

He pulled a dark red silk robe from a chair and put it on.

'My God.' Jenna studied it, frowning. 'That looks familiar.'

'It should. You gave it to me our first Christmas together.'

She wrinkled her nose. 'Actually, our only Christmas together. I'm amazed you kept it.'

'I kept everything that had the slightest connection with you,' he said quietly. 'I think my worst moment was finding your wedding ring, pushed into a bag. It was like hearing my own death knell being sounded. Yet there it is— back where it belongs.'

Jenna lay back against the pillows, folding her arms behind her head. 'So,' she said, giving him a deliberately provocative look from under her lashes, 'what am I going to wear?'

Ross laughed. 'Do I get to choose? Because what you have on now is incredibly becoming.'

'Not if I'm covered in goosebumps,' she retorted. 'These old cottages can get very chilly in the evenings.'

'I could supply a remedy for that, too.' Ross gave her a mock leer, then reached into the wardrobe and produced one of his shirts. 'But as an alternative will this do?'

There were two fillet steaks in the fridge, which they grilled and ate along with tiny new potatoes and a tomato salad. They drank Rioja.

Afterwards they made coffee, and drank it in the living room, sitting on the rug next to the fire, which he had coaxed back to life.

And later, as she sat in the circle of his arms, watching the flames and listening to Debussy's *La Mer* on the hi-fi system, she said softly, 'I'm still hungry.'

'For food?'

'No.'

'Ah,' he said, and began, without haste, to unfasten the buttons on the shirt.

This time his lovemaking was unhurried, too, as he attended to all her wants with exquisite and tantalising finesse, his own pleasures subjected to hers, bringing her over and over again to the brink of climax before he allowed her the ultimate release, muffling her sobbing, enraptured cry with his kiss.

And then it was her turn to please him, using her hands and mouth with voluptuous joy, as she knew he liked her to do. Reviving a thousand passionate, sensuous memories. Until he lifted himself over her and entered her again, to take them both soaring to a new universe that was theirs alone.

Afterwards Ross wrapped his arms around her. He said softly, 'Would you think me very unromantic if I suggested we went up to bed and got some sleep?'

'Not at all.' Jenna burrowed against him. 'I haven't had a full night's rest since I saw you on Trevarne Head.'

She felt him smile against her hair. 'Now, that's a pattern I intend to continue,' he said. 'But for more enjoyable reasons.'

'Really?' Jenna trailed a fingertip down his chest. 'Would you care to provide details?'

'I'd be delighted,' Ross said courteously. 'At some more convenient moment. In the meantime, we have a wedding to attend tomorrow, and it won't look good if we suddenly keel over and start snoring in the middle of the ceremony. Apart from mortifying Christy, we'd probably give Betty Fox a heart attack.'

'I expect she'll have one anyway, when word gets out. You realise we'll be her sole topic of conversation for the foreseeable future?'

'Well,' he said, 'we won't be around to hear it.'

'You don't want us to remarry in the parish church.'

'I want to marry you,' he said, 'with a special licence, in London, as soon as it can be arranged. But we'll come back here for the christening.' He ran a questing hand the length of her body and sighed regretfully. 'Now, up with you, minx. Put the spark guard in front of the fire while I lock up.'

'Yes, my lord,' Jenna said demurely, doing a little questing on her own account, then jumping up and running off, laughing as he reached for her.

Once they were in bed Ross went to sleep almost at once, one arm thrown protectively across her body. But Jenna stayed awake for a little while, for the sheer joy of feeling his weight next to her and hearing his quiet, steady breathing.

It was true, she thought, marvelling. Love did conquer all. It had fought pain and bitterness and recrimination, and won triumphantly. And she and Ross were both the victors.

When she did finally close her eyes, her rest was quiet and dreamless.

Even through the waves of sleep that still engulfed her, Jenna was aware that something was wrong. That a noise was intruding upon her consciousness.

She forced open unwilling eyelids and listened. Someone, she realised without pleasure, seemed to be knocking on the front door.

Thirza must have decided not to stay at Trevarne House after all, she thought, making use of Ross's shirt again and buttoning it more decorously this time.

He hadn't stirred, of course, and she bent, dropping a wry kiss on his hair before treading barefoot out of the room and down the stairs.

The pounding on the door hadn't abated at all. Indeed, it seemed to have increased in impatience.

'Hold on, I'm coming,' she called, as she took the key from its hook and turned it in the massive lock.

As the door opened her brows snapped together in a frown of sheer incredulity as she saw who was standing on the doorstep.

'Natasha?' She shook her head in bewilderment. 'What are you doing here?'

'I drove down. I was worried about you—about the situation here. And how right I was.' Natasha's eyes, burning like hot coals, travelled over Jenna's half-clad body. 'Very fetching.' She used the words like daggers. 'I was on my way up to Trevarne when I met this man coming away—Adrian something. Christy's intended, I suppose. He told me you were down here—and why.' She paused. 'Well, aren't you going to invite me in? I've had a hell of a journey.'

'Tasha.' Jenna hesitated, feeling embarrassed and self-conscious. 'This isn't my house. I can't really invite you to stay here.' She wanted to feel sorry about that, because Natasha really did look tired, her face strained and her skin sallow. She knew she should be more welcoming, but somehow it was impossible.

'I don't want to stay,' Natasha said curtly. 'I want you to get in the car and come back to London with me. Now. Before you make an even more abject fool of yourself over Ross Grantham.'

Her mouth twisted contemptuously. 'I see he's managed to get you into bed. But, then, that's his speciality, isn't it? Giving women a wonderful, unforgettable time sexually. A one way ticket to Paradise. And I suppose it's a novelty—doing it with his ex-wife. But don't fool yourself, Jenna. The novelty will soon wear off, and he'll be on to the next lucky girl in line.'

She was in the hall by this time, pushing the heavy door shut behind her, and Jenna found herself wanting to take a step backwards.

Don't be stupid, she adjured herself silently. You're half awake and off-balance, that's all.

Aloud, she said gently, 'Natasha—it isn't what you think.'

'Wrong.' Natasha walked past her into the living room, switching on the wall lamps and undoing her trench coat. 'Wrong. It's exactly what I think. Because you have that look about you again—that sleek, cat-that-got-the-cream look that I always hated. There were times when you came sneaking back at dawn when I swear I could smell him on you.'

She drew a breath, eyes half closed. 'That unique clean scent of his skin, mixed up with that cologne he always used.'

Jenna began to feel cold in a way that had no connection with her admittedly scanty covering, or the temperature of the room.

This was a deep, bone-aching chill that she knew of old. And it was called fear.

'I suppose I can't really blame you,' Natasha went on, almost conversationally. 'You have been celibate for some time, and Ross is a marvellous lay. Why shouldn't you indulge yourself—have some fun? But now it's time to wake up to reality again, my pet. You finished with Ross. You divorced him because he was blatantly and cruelly unfaithful. As he's always been. And as he always will be.' She shrugged. 'I don't think he can help himself.'

Jenna made a small sound and Natasha stared at her. 'Why, Jenna, sweetie, you've gone quite pale.' She giggled. 'What's the matter, pussy cat? Has your cream suddenly gone sour?'

Jenna steadied herself. Any moment now, she thought, I'm going to wake up and find this whole thing has been a nightmare.

She said quietly, 'I'm not going back to London until after the wedding, Natasha. And when I do Ross will be with me. We're getting married again.'

'Why, yes.' Natasha sounded amused. 'Adrian, the bridegroom to be mentioned something of the kind. But it's all nonsense, you know, Jenna. Ross and marriage simply don't work. And you can't take him back just because he's fabulous in the sack. All serial womanisers are. It's their stock in trade.'

'Thank you,' Ross said politely, 'for the un-expected testimonial. But then, Natasha, you're always so—unexpected.'

Neither of them had been aware of his approach. He was also barefoot, wrapped in the red silk robe, leaning against the door frame. He was smiling, but his eyes were black ice.

He said, 'To what do we owe this—signal honour?'

'Jenna is my best friend,' Natasha flung at him through taut lips. 'Also my business part-ner. I came to rescue her.'

'How very dramatic of you,' Ross drawled. 'I wasn't aware that she needed rescuing.'

'Oh, but she does,' Natasha said, nodding. 'She really does. From a love rat like you.'

'You have a nice turn of phrase,' he said. 'If the art game ever palls, you could get a job on a tabloid newspaper.'

'Don't you laugh at me.' Her voice shook with some suppressed emotion. 'Don't you dare laugh.'

'Please believe that I find nothing even remotely amusing in this situation.' Ross straightened and took a step into the room, tightening the sash of his robe. He said, 'Jenna, darling, haven't you offered your best friend and business partner some refreshment after she's driven all this way in the middle of the night?' He tutted reprovingly. 'How remiss of you, when she's been to all this trouble. And on your behalf, too.' He paused. 'Or did you ask her to come?'

Jenna said tonelessly, 'I didn't invite her, and I don't know why she's here.'

His brows lifted. 'You mean she just—turned up?'

'She telephoned this afternoon just before the rehearsal. I—I told her that you were here, and that it had brought back a lot of memories I'd thought buried. But I never asked her for help.'

She hesitated, then went on, her voice faltering a little. 'Ross—she's been saying—hinting at—things. I need you to tell me they're not true.'

'Only hinting? You surprise me.' He looked at Natasha, his face hardening. 'You have your captive audience. Why not open the whole can of worms? Or are you waiting for me to tell Jenna that we once slept together?'

Jenna took a step backwards, her hand flying to her mouth. 'Oh, no.' It was a moan. 'Please—no.'

'Unfortunately, yes. But it was before I met you again. And I had no idea that she was your flatmate, or that she even knew you.'

'Why—why did you not say—something?'

'Because I don't kiss and tell. Also, I didn't see what possible good it would do. I thought she would feel the same, but I was wrong.'

'Oh, yes,' Natasha said huskily. 'Wrong about so many things. You really thought you could become my lover, then drop me—*me*—when something better came along?'

'Natasha,' he said. 'We had sex together—once. Not a raging affair.'

Natasha swung round to Jenna, her face gloating. 'I was there first, Jenna. How does that make you feel? I was before you in that beautiful riverside apartment of his. Before you in his bed.'

'Oh, God,' Jenna whispered. 'Oh, dear God.'

Ross came over to her. He took her hand and held it tightly. 'Jenna, listen to me. I met Natasha at a party. We started talking, and as we were leaving I asked if she'd like to go for a drink. We went to a bar, and then back to my place. She said all the right things, made all the right moves, but I already knew it was a mistake.

'So I made noises about a heavy day tomorrow and offered to get her a cab. She asked if she could use the bathroom. She was gone for such a long time I thought she'd been taken ill. I found her in my room, stretched across the bed without a stitch on. She looked spectacular, and it seemed—churlish to disappoint her. Another big mistake. When it was over I called the cab and she disappeared—out of my life, I thought. But I was wrong.'

'Don't listen to him,' Natasha said, smiling. 'He seduced me. He couldn't keep his hands off me. He wanted me to stay the night.'

His voice was ice. 'Believe me, Natasha, that was the last thing I wanted.'

He turned back to Jenna. 'She hadn't wasted her time in the apartment. She'd taken my phone number, mobile number, and even the name of the agency.' He sighed impatiently. 'I began to get daily calls. She wanted to come round and cook me a meal. She had theatre tickets. There was this film she was dying to see. A couple of times I came out of the agency and found her outside. She said she happened to be passing, but I began to feel hunted—as if I was being stalked. And I was beginning to run out of excuses as to why I couldn't see her.'

'But you did see me again,' Natasha said. She sounded complacent, almost triumphant, as if nothing he'd been saying had impinged on her. 'I asked you to the private view at the gallery and you came.'

'Yes,' he said. 'I planned to take you to dinner afterwards and tell you as gently as possible that it wouldn't work in a hundred years, to ask you not to call me again.'

He looked at Jenna, his eyes softening. 'But then I saw you, my love, and everything else went out of my head. Everything but the need to be with you, and you only.'

He paused. 'I intended to call Natasha, to apologise and explain, but she called me first. I'd expected her to be angry, but I wasn't prepared for the tirade of hysterical abuse that hit me. She'd got it into her head that we were into some on-going relationship and that I'd jilted her.

'And then it stopped, as if she'd thrown a switch, and she was all sweetness and light and being incredibly understanding about me being a man who couldn't keep his bloody zip fastened. I think she even forgave me at one point, and said we'd start again. I told her that we wouldn't. That I was involved, and in love. And she went very quiet. When she spoke again, she said it was far from over between us, and that unless I accepted it she'd make me sorry.

'I told her I was already sorrier than she could have ever dreamed, and rang off.'

Jenna said, 'But that wasn't the end of it—was it? I heard her on the office phone once. She must have been talking to you.'

'Probably,' he said. 'Unless she had a whole series of us staked out across London.' He put an arm round Jenna and drew her close. He said, 'And then the anonymous calls started. And all that other stuff.'

Natasha said thickly, 'You can't prove a thing.'

'It was your scent on the handkerchief, and the shirt,' Ross said. 'I recognised it at once, because it was one I'd never liked and you were wearing it at that party.'

'Tigresse,' Jenna whispered. She stared at Natasha. Her friend. Her business partner. A woman with a stranger's face. 'Your special occasion scent. Why didn't I recognise it?'

'Because you had no reason to make the connection,' Ross said grimly. 'But I did. And you worked with her, invited her to the house, so it was easy for her to plant the evidence.'

'Oh, Natasha.' Jenna's voice broke. 'How could you?'

'Because I wanted him.' The older woman's voice throbbed with bitterness. 'I could have made him happy if he'd just given me a chance, and instead I had to stand there and watch him walk off with you. I swore I'd make you both sorry, and I did.'

The look she sent Jenna was sly, almost gleeful. 'Even I never imagined how success- ful I'd be at that.'

'So what brought you here tonight?' Ross asked quietly. 'The need to make more trou- ble—to convince Jenna that I was just a worth- less, womanising bastard who'd break her heart all over again? Or did it go deeper than that? Was it her admission that being with me had stimulated all kinds of lost memories that made you come running?'

Natasha threw her head back haughtily. 'I don't know what you're talking about.'

'I think you do,' Ross said. 'I've always thought so. Always had this terrible suspicion that maybe Jenna's fall in the gallery that day wasn't as accidental as it was made out to be.' He studied her with narrowed, inimical eyes. 'After all, you were alone together when it happened.'

'Ross,' Jenna intervened, troubled. 'I think that's taking things too far. Tasha was nowhere near me when I tripped.'

'Is that what you did?' He held her shoul- ders, looking deeply into her eyes. 'On one of the few occasions I could get you to talk about it, you said you'd slipped. That's a very different thing. So which was it, Jenna?'

'You want her to remember that?' Natasha spat at him. 'The worst day of her life? Don't do this, Jenna. You'll only distress yourself.'

'I think it's a little late for you to worry about that,' Ross said harshly. 'But that's why you're here, isn't it. Because you're terrified that among all the other memories she might recall just how she came to fall that day.'

Jenna was very still. 'I didn't trip,' she said. 'I was going down the stairs, carrying a picture, and I stood on something—something that rolled under my foot—and I—went forward.'

'A pencil?' Ross said. 'Or a pen, perhaps? Which was it, Natasha?'

She stared at him, her eyes glittering. 'Are you completely mad? I was the one who looked after her. Who got the ambulance when I realised she was bleeding.'

'By which time it was too late, of course.' Ross sounded bleak, and unutterably weary.

Jenna detached herself gently from his clasp and went over to Natasha. She said, 'Tell me—please tell me you didn't do this. That you didn't put something on the stairs, hoping that I'd fall.'

'Pride always comes before a fall.' Natasha was breathing hoarsely, her breasts rising and falling swiftly. 'And you were so proud, Jenna, so pleased that you were carrying that bastard's child. Everything you needed to make your happiness complete, you said. Everything I was never going to have.

'And I hated you for that. For making him love you. For taking him away from me—*me*. And for having his baby.' She shook her head slowly. 'I—really couldn't allow that...'

She smiled almost reminiscently. 'It wasn't anything that I'd planned. I could see you were having trouble on the stairs, and I decided to help that on a little. There was a piece of dowel in the office, and I put it one of the steps.' She shrugged. 'After that, it was in the lap of the gods.

'You could have missed it completely. And there was a moment when I almost stopped you. Because I always liked you, Jenna. It was only Ross that came between us. Once he was out of the way, we could be friends again. And we were.' Her smile was placid, almost childlike. 'Weren't we?'

'Yes,' Jenna said, breaking the appalled silence. She was shivering. 'Yes, we were. You were—good to me.'

'I needed to make amends,' Natasha said, making it sound totally reasonable. 'It's a terrible thing to lose a baby.' Her face seemed to shrink, become much older. 'Almost as bad as never having one.'

'Natasha.' Jenna's voice rang with pain. 'Don't. You'll meet someone—who'll love you...' And she faltered into silence, because she knew it wasn't true.

Natasha was too damaged, too unstable ever to sustain a relationship. She needed help, and maybe had done so for a very long time.

'But I wanted Ross,' Natasha said simply. 'And now you have him—again.'

Her hand came out of her pocket, holding a small sharp knife, and she lunged towards Jenna, her face twisted, almost unrecognisable. Only Ross was there first, grabbing her, seizing the hand that held the knife and forcing her to drop it. Holding her until she stopped struggling.

For a moment there was silence, then a new sound filled the room—the noise of weeping, huge tearing sobs interspersed with small animal cries, and Natasha sank down to the carpet, curling herself into a small, defensive ball, her hands covering her face and her whole body shaking.

Ross looked across at Jenna, who was standing, white-faced and wide-eyed, her hand pressed to her throat, still trying to comprehend everything she had seen and heard.

He said gently, 'Darling, you have to ring for an ambulance—and the police. Can you do that? I think I should stay here—keep an eye on her.'

She stirred, said in a low voice, 'Does it have to be the police?'

'Yes,' he said. 'This whole thing has gone far enough. She's a danger—not just to us, but to herself. We can't let it pass.'

When the emergency services arrived Natasha was relatively calm again and sitting in a chair. 'It's so kind of you all,' she kept saying. 'So kind of you to help me.'

Jenna couldn't bear to watch her being taken away, so she escaped into the kitchen. Where Ross found her, sitting at the kitchen table, her hands folded in her lap, staring into space.

She said, 'I was going to make some coffee, but I couldn't open the jar.'

'I'll do it,' he said. 'And I'll get us both some brandy, too. I think we need it.'

'Yes,' she said. She swallowed. 'Ross—that was so awful. Because that was the vegetable knife she had with her. Something I've used myself in the kitchen when we shared a flat.' She shuddered. 'I—I still can't really believe any of this. That she could do these things...'

'Nor I,' he said quietly. 'Even though I did have my suspicions about her from the first. There was something odd about her—something that warned me to steer clear. I know Seb felt it, too, when we had them over for dinner.' He shrugged, his face cynical. 'But she had a beautiful body, and I was fool enough to be tempted.'

'Why didn't you tell me that you knew her?' Jenna asked quietly. 'That you'd been to bed with her?'

His mouth tightened painfully. 'I meant to—and I should have done, as soon as I realised how close you were to her. But we had only just got together, darling, and what we had was all so new—so fragile. I was afraid of damaging our own relationship. And later—it never seemed the right time, apart from being a pretty unsavoury incident.

'I hoped, you see, that I was wrong about her. That she'd find herself a man of her own and the whole thing could be quietly forgotten.' He shook his head. 'Only she had other ideas.'

Jenna shivered. 'What will happen to her?'

'I've no idea. I suppose the whole mental health machinery will swing into action. We'll have to make statements at some point.' He paused. 'Did she have any family?'

'I don't know,' Jenna said slowly. 'She never talked about them. I suppose I should have realised that was—strange.' She sighed. 'And I shared a flat with her—a place of work. I should have known. I feel as if I'm to blame...'

'No, Jenna.' Ross knelt beside her chair, capturing her hands firmly in his. 'You must never think that. I am certain that whatever was wrong with Natasha began a long time ago, before she met either of us, although I suspect I might have been the catalyst.'

She said quietly, 'Poor Natasha.'

'You can say that?' Ross's brows snapped together. 'My darling, she could have killed you that day in the gallery. And tonight she tried to stab you—do you serious damage. And you can still feel sorry for her?'

'Yes.' She freed one hand, so that she could touch his face. Stroke his hair. Reassure herself that her own personal miracle had really happened.

Her smile was wavering, but it was a smile just the same, and her eyes were shining with everything she felt for him. 'Because we have everything. And she has nothing.'

Ross bent his head, and put his lips against her bare knee. 'Yes,' he said. 'My one and only love. We have everything. Poor Natasha.'

It had been a wonderful wedding. Everyone was agreed on that. The weather was perfect, the bride looked radiant, and the reception was going with a swing.

The bridesmaid, it was felt, looked a little pale, but there were rumours flying about some fuss in the village the previous night.

'One of they stalkers,' Betty Fox said with relish. 'Terrible, they are, by all accounts.' Her tone suggested it would provide valuable material to chew over in the days to come. 'Still, no harm done,' she added with faint regret.

Ross had dealt with the celebratory messages with charm and aplomb, and now he was rising with a glass in his hand.

'Ladies and gentlemen,' he said. 'This is the moment when it's my duty as best man to propose the health of the bridesmaid. But on this occasion I'm combining it with another toast. So, will you please rise and drink with me to Jenna, and to the happiness of my once and future wife.'

Jenna sat, flushed and laughing, amid the surprised cries and smug smiles. Christy and Adrian were the first on their feet, glasses raised. Further down the table she could see Thirza nodding wisely, and Aunt Grace dabbing at her eyes with a lace handkerchief.

And when the dancing began she and Ross were applauded warmly as they followed the bride and groom on to the floor.

'Happy?' Ross whispered, holding her closely.

'More than you will ever know.' She looked into his eyes, afraid no longer. Knowing what she would see there. Glorying in the passion, the tenderness and the need.

And in the certainty of a love that would last for the rest of their lives.